The Forty-Niners

Center Point
Large Print

**This Large Print Book carries the
Seal of Approval of N.A.V.H.**

WEST OF THE BIG RIVER

The Forty-Niners

*A Novel Based on
the California Gold Seekers*

CHARLIE STEEL

CENTER POINT LARGE PRINT
THORNDIKE, MAINE

This Center Point Large Print edition
is published in the year 2021 by arrangement with
Western Fictioneers.

The text of this Large Print edition is unabridged.
In other aspects, this book may vary
from the original edition.
Printed in the United States of America
on permanent paper.
Set in 16-point Times New Roman type.

ISBN: 978-1-63808-017-6

The Library of Congress has cataloged this record
under Library of Congress Control Number: 2021936986

The
Forty-Niners

CHAPTER ONE

Slavery, the harsh, cruel, and meanest kind, existed since the beginning of man. In 1772, St. Louis, Missouri recorded 198 slaves—by 1849, nearly 6000. Decades of relations with Indian, Spanish and Negro slaves produced children who looked more like their white masters than the original slaves. It was only strict laws and documented births that kept these white-skinned children slaves. Once escaped into the populace, no one was aware what blood coursed through the veins of those individuals. And, since the outside appearance of man was judged, and blood could not be, no one knew.

Except for the escaped slave.

Lance, a white-skinned young man, had all he could take of slavery, and despite the penalty of death, was ready to run. The hovel Lance escaped from could be compared to that of a rat's nest. Some would say not even a rat would have resided in such a place. Forced up early in the morning, fed a breakfast of dirty half-cooked gruel, he was sent into the fields to work the earth. It was the overseer who wielded the whip. The master in his home was often unaware and unconcerned.

Lance was twenty-one when he ran. He escaped,

and the many slave patrols that roamed the city, those ruthless men who enforced the slave laws, ran after him—chasing him down like the dog they considered him to be. In fact, it was with dogs that he was tracked. His description went out: twenty-one, muscular, over six feet tall, light skinned with green eyes, and a crown of curling straw-colored hair. How such a splendid product of humanity could be produced from a slave hovel with so little decent food was a miracle of nature. For Lance towered above most men, his scarred back a glorious construction of muscle and sinew. Lance was a living example of what Greek statues were meant to represent, a perfect reflection of the very best attributes of man.

There was only one place Lance could run to escape the noses of the dogs and the slave patrols—the Mississippi River. As he ran, the young man passed by one of the many well-displayed slave signs:

**By order of the City of St. Louis,
all Slaves are forbidden to do the following:**

**Ride in a carriage—without permission
Walk with a cane
Make seditious speeches
Meet in church without white observers
Smoke in public
Read or Write**

**The State of Missouri does not recognize marriage between slaves.
All Slaves and Free Blacks must possess a pass at all times.
Violators face penalty of capture, whippings, or death.**

Lance could not read, but he knew what the sign said, that because he was a slave he had no rights or freedom—not even the freedom of a free-roaming mongrel dog. Today, he chose to gain the rights of a human being, he would run and fight to be allowed to live without another man having ownership over him.

He decided that he would rather die than exist another day in captivity.

Katherine Day and her son Johnny were busy in the kitchen. Her father and her two uncles, Harold and Clare, had taken a load of vegetables to market and wouldn't return until late evening. The three brothers owned adjoining farms and worked the land together. Katherine, known as Katy, finished peeling potatoes and put them in the pot of water on the stove. She was making supper, and tonight they would have rabbit stew with carrots and mashed potatoes. Her elders would return hungry, and if she didn't make large portions, the men would complain.

It was the twenty-ninth of August, 1848, and a

hot summer day. A breeze blew in from a south-west window Katy had left open, and the white curtain fluttered. Katy stooped to check the bread in the oven, then rose and went to a kitchen chair to rest for a moment. Despite what her father said, cooking was hard work. It was warm, too warm; the fire in the cook stove further heated the house.

It was about this time last year the fever epidemic came, Katy reflected. It claimed her mother, her husband Jack, her uncles's wives, and their children. Uncle Harold took it hard when he lost his wife and son and daughter. He started drinking and had been no good to anyone for the past twelve months. He was just now coming out of it.

Uncle Clare reacted differently. He never really discussed the loss of his wife and two girls. Katy wondered sometimes why Uncle Clare didn't talk. Perhaps the pain was too great. Or maybe that was just how some people coped. Once the funerals were over he went back to working the farm, not saying a word about the epidemic, the loss of family, or of all those other towns-people and farm families who had died.

For Katy there was guilt which she shared with no one. Her father was in some ways a hard and unsympathetic man. It was he who had forced her to marry Jack—a man she really did not want. A drifter, Jack had come to the farm as a working hand, and it wasn't long before he began courting her. Katy's father and uncles pushed her to marry. After a long while she succumbed to the pressure.

That was nearly six years ago. It turned out that Jack was an abusive man. The cabin her family built for them was on the back forty. It stood empty now, and barren, a thing of the past.

Katy was unaware of it, but her son Johnny stared at his mother, wondering what made her look so far away. At the moment, Katy sat missing her mother and remembering her warmth and her smiling face. She would give anything to have her back, once again helping with the meal as she had so many times. Her mother had been supportive when her father and uncles had not. Guiltily, Katy thought of her husband Jack, and realized she had no feelings of loss toward the man who had fathered her child.

"Mommy," said Johnny, who was sitting on the floor playing with a toy wagon, "are you alright?"

She was so deep in thought it took a moment for Katy to react. When she did, she smiled at her son.

"I'm okay, Johnny. I was just thinking of the past."

"You miss Grandma?" asked the child.

"Why yes, I do."

"And Daddy?"

"Him too," lied Katy.

She returned to her cooking and when the

dinner was fully prepared, she set the table and waited. At the time she expected, the front door of the cabin burst open and the first one through the door was her father and he was full of unusual enthusiasm.

"Guess what, girl?" boomed her father's voice. "Old man Fuller gave us a copy of the *New York Herald*."

"Yes?"

"They discovered gold in Californy! Daughter . . . what do you think of that?"

"I don't know . . . what am I supposed to think?"

"Why, they say folks are picking nuggets off the ground. Your uncles and I discussed it and soon as we sell our farms and outfit our wagons, we'll be heading west!"

"Father, you've been wanting to do that since before Mother died."

The uncles had come through the door, and when they heard mention of death, their enthusiasm waned. The smiles of the men disappeared.

"Besides," said Katy, practical as ever, "you can't go to California or over the mountains in the winter."

"Doggone if she ain't right," said Uncle Harold. "I didn't think of that."

"Well!" pronounced Katy's father. "I won't let my daughter put a damper on this. First thing in spring, we load our wagons and head out."

"If you sell the farms," reminded Katy.

There were frowns from the men and extended silence.

"I'll be glad to go, Grandpa," said Johnny, who had risen to his feet, his toy wagon still in his hand.

"That's the spirit I want to hear!" beamed Peter Day.

"That food smells great, Katy!" exclaimed Uncle Clare. "Suppose we fill our bellies before talking more of this Californy business."

When word came to Red Jennings and his partner Jake Vargas that gold was discovered in California, they began preparing for the trip. The men ran a general store in St. Louis. Independence, Missouri, the jumping off place for the California and Oregon Trail, was just across the state. They immediately purchased wagons and began to pick supplies to take with them. Their idea from the start was to form a company of men to share the work of prospecting and digging for gold. Share and share alike was their motto, and they posted signs in the store for partners.

On December 5, 1848, President James Polk announced to Congress that the gold discovery in California was real. When this news hit the papers, Red and Jake had no trouble getting signatures from fifteen men who signed an agreement. They called themselves the St. Louis

Gold Association. Seventeen men would travel together to the California gold fields, sharing equipment, work, and proceeds from all gold found. The buy-in was fifteen hundred dollars—a steep price at the time, but this paid for wagons, mules, and all supplies, furnished, of course, by Red and Jake. Since it was now December, they would continue to run their store until spring. On the first of April, they would begin their jump off from Independence and head out on the California Trail.

CHAPTER TWO

Many armed patrols enthusiastically policed the six thousand slaves in St. Louis. A slave party, mounted on horseback, with its dogs, took up the scent of Lance and chased after him. The young man had all he could take and he ran as fast as his body would allow, flexing well-used muscles formed from twenty-one years of hard labor. Lance saw the river and ran for it. Into its muddy depths he flung himself, just as the gaping jaws of many toothed mouths were ready to close. The slavers stopped their horses at the Mississippi River's edge and waited for the curly haired young man's head to rise.

There was a wind and the water was choppy; he would be hard to spot. Lance had a chest and lungs unequalled by any man in the state of Missouri and today he used them. He held his breath and swam through the murky depths. Far out he raised his head for a breath and went under again. Concealed by a wave, the slavers never saw him. Not once was a rifle or pistol fired.

Not even a man as strong as Lance could fight the mighty currents of the Mississippi without succumbing to its power. It was to a dangling rope on a small sailing scow that the young man clung. When his breath came back, he climbed the rope, and dripping wet, hoisted himself to his feet upon the deck of the ship. Then he walked to the stern to be spotted by the owner, who held a wooden tiller under one arm and a cup of coffee in the other hand.

"The Saints be praised," exclaimed the Irishman, putting down the cup and crossing himself, "if it ain't the glory of Adonis himself!"

Lance stood in wet, thread-bare clothing that stretched tightly across his muscular frame. Every muscle was clearly outlined through a nearly transparent shirt, and snug-fitting pants. He did look like a living picture of Adonis—a figure of Greek mythology he had never seen or even heard of.

"My name's not Adonis, it's Lance. I'm hitching a ride and I won't cause trouble if you don't cause me none."

"Glory be! I'll not be sending you to the depths. I'd rather fling my own son overboard than the likes of you. Welcome aboard and if you be wanting work, I pay fair wages."

"What work would that be?" asked Lance.

"Why, man, I'm sailing freight and supplies up and down the river. I never saw a better piece of equipment than you for loading and unloading. My last man up and quit on me and my ten-year-old son, who sleeps below, hardly fits the bill."

"I'll take the job," said Lance without hesitation.

"Good! Good! First port of call is up the river a ways. We have barrels of molasses, sacks of rice and flour. Half the boat to unload, if you think you're up to it."

"I can do four men's work," said Lance, with no intent of bragging.

"I believe you, lad, I believe you. Come sit! I'll pour you a cup of coffee, and cook up a few eggs, some hash, with bread and cheese and try to fill that belly of yours. But first, here's a blanket to wrap around you to dry you off and keep you warm."

It didn't take long for Peter, Harold, and Clare Day to find buyers. By October, all three farms were sold with the agreement they wouldn't have to vacate until spring. The sale didn't include the stock, which they would keep until spring and sell when the price was highest. All winter the men discussed gold prospecting. They bought a book on the subject and began to collect tools and anticipated making a rocker or a Long Tom. Each had a sturdy farm wagon, and these they worked on and reinforced. They made canopies for the wagons, and by March they sold their stock, and were fully loaded and ready to go. Their farms were located near Indianapolis, Indiana, and they would have to cross half of Indiana, Illinois, and all of Missouri to get to Independence. They were anxious to get started, and it was in a blowing snowstorm they began their long trip.

"Why do you make us freeze?" complained Katy. "Johnny is wrapped in three blankets and still his teeth are chattering."

"Just like a woman," growled her father, who held the reins of the first wagon. "We want to get there before all the good claims are taken. It'll be more than five months. Every minute on the trail counts."

That first night they slept in their wagons and almost succumbed to the cold; the same for the second, third, and fourth day. Johnny came down with a fever, and it took all of Katy's skill to care for the child. The three brothers still would not stop and they drove across Indiana into Illinois. For days they traveled, camping alongside the road. They were now on the main route to St. Louis and there were many travelers. Katy was surprised that most seemed to have the same destination, the gold fields in California.

One night they put up camp and Katy went about fixing supper. She was boiling beans and frying beef to add to the pot. The three brothers went to visit a wagon parked close by, and when dinner was ready, her father and uncles returned with two young men.

"Meet Joe and Frank Sparks," said her father.

"Hello," said Katy, not in the best of moods.

"I invited them for supper," exclaimed her

father. "They're going to be prospectors just like us!"

"Father," the daughter protested. "We barely have enough for ourselves."

"Don't mind her," said Peter Day. "You men pick up a plate and dish up. Katy makes a mighty fine meal, if I do say so myself. Umm, smells good. Beans and meat."

The five men lined up and it wasn't long before they were scraping the pot. Katy dished up a small bowl for Johnny, and she spooned the bottom, finding a meager portion for herself. Eying the men warily, Katy sat on a wagon tongue some distance from the boisterous group. All they talked about was gold and California. She was more than tired of it. Being on the trail day and night would be a burden she did not want to think about. Thank goodness the weather had turned warmer.

"You say you two are heading for Independence?" asked Peter Day.

"That's right," replied Joe Sparks.

"And you were both farmers in Indiana?"

"That's right," responded Frank, his brother.

"I'm taking a shine to you two young fellers," said Peter. "Suppose you join up with us and we travel together to Californy?"

"We wouldn't want to put upon you," said Joe.

"No such problem," replied Peter. "We can share in the cost of vittles and Katy won't mind cooking up for two more. Would you, Katy?"

The men looked at the young mother, and instead of replying, she merely shook her head.

Now there were four wagons, five men, a young woman, and a little boy. Traveling across Illinois they came near to the mighty Mississippi. They turned off the main road in a downpour and followed a smaller lane where they camped for the night. Finding fewer travelers, they decided to continue on the lesser road. By evening they drove to the mouth of the Dubois River which flowed into the Mississippi. The four wagons parked near a wharf where a small sailing scow was tied to the dock. There, the travelers watched a gigantic young man unloading cargo. The fellow effortlessly lifted barrels of molasses, and sacks of rice and flour which he loaded onto a waiting wagon. The young man carried a double load from the boat, and he made it look easy.

"Now there's a fellow to have with us," exclaimed Peter.

Katy, despite herself, could not help but stare. Not only was the young man bulging with muscles, but he was also splendidly handsome. She, along with the three brothers, watched this magnificent display of strength and agility.

Captain Kelly O'Reilly and his son Sean were standing near the wagon. The sailor responded to Katy's father.

"Just took that fellow on a while back," said

Captain O'Reilly. "They'll be no way I'll let you be taking the best crewman I ever hired."

"I don't think I've seen a stronger man in all my life," commented Peter Day. "Now, can you help us find a place to ferry across the river?"

"Why sure, be glad to give you directions," replied Captain O'Reilly.

Red Jennings, Jake Vargas, and the fifteen men of the St. Louis Gold Association were all set to leave so they would arrive at Independence by April 1st. They were held up when the deal on selling the general store fell through. It took another agonizing two weeks before they found a buyer, and every day the men complained to Red.

Finally, the second week in April they started out. They traveled from St. Louis with eight wagons fully loaded with food and supplies. When they reached Independence, the California Trail was already heavily trodden with thousands of gold seekers. Red's gold mining party left a month late and didn't arrive at Fort Kearny until mid-June. They had pushed their mules hard and it showed. As they drove towards the fort, a frontiersman dressed in buckskins and fur hat and holding a rifle, stood near the entrance and commented to Red up on the lead wagon.

"Keep pushing those mules like that and you'll never make Californy."

Red's reply showed his anger and frustration. "I suppose you could do better!"

"I could," replied the plainsman. "I've made the trip often enough. In fact, I helped Kit Carson guide Fremont on his last expedition to Oregon."

The wagons halted, and the men heard the comments of the old-timer.

"You wouldn't be interested in guiding us?" asked Red, now standing before the plainsman. "My name's Red, this here is my partner, Jake. And these fellers you see are part of the St. Louis Gold Association. We aim to share in all the gold we dig up."

"Folks call me Horntoad Harry. If you men will pay me for guiding ya, I'd be right willing."

"Why don't you join our association?"

"I don't much care for diggin' in the dirt. I done it afore and it ain't likely I'll do it again."

"Then how much?" asked Red.

"How about five hunnerd?"

"Suppose we talk some more on this, and then give us a chance to decide," replied Red.

"Don't take too long," replied Horntoad Harry. "Another group just might snatch me up."

CHAPTER THREE

For three more weeks Lance worked for the Irishman, loading and unloading the boat with an exchange of supplies and money for the owner. For the first time in his life, Lance made close acquaintances with two people, Kelly O'Reilly, the captain of the scow, and his son, Sean. But when the captain talked of heading back to St. Louis, Lance quit his job.

"But, son," said Captain O'Reilly. "You've just started, you do such grand work, and we get along so famously."

"I cannot go back to that place," said Lance, shaking his head.

"But why?"

"I won't say."

"If it's the trouble with the law, I'll . . ." began O'Reilly.

"What good am I if I can't do the work?" said Lance. "You need me to load and unload and St. Louis is poison to me."

O'Reilly gave the lad twenty dollars. It was fair pay. The captain couldn't let the best worker he ever had go without coin. Over his ragged clothing Lance now wore an old canvas coat. He departed at Davenport, Iowa, after finishing loading supplies off and on the boat. As the scow sailed away, Lance waved from the dock to

O'Reilly and his son, and the captain called back to him.

"Good luck to you, lad, and may the Saints protect you!"

Lance, knowing nothing of the Catholic religion, had little knowledge of what Saints he referred to. Walking down the dock, he took no more than fifty steps before he was hailed by a large brute of a man.

"If you're looking for work, there's freight to unload."

Going aboard a steam packet, Lance began carrying crates, casks, and hundred-pound sacks and placing them on wagon beds as ordered. By the end of the day, he had carried three times the freight of the other men. When the big man came to be paid, he was given less coin than men who did a third of the work.

"Why do you cheat me?" asked Lance.

"If you don't like it, try taking it out of my hide," challenged the dock foreman.

Lance took hold of the big man and raised him bodily over his head. The dock foreman, a fighter all his life, tried in vain to halt the action. He found himself flung off the platform and into the water as if a child. Men who had suffered blows and verbal abuse from the bully cheered Lance on. Then the muscular young man walked off the wharf and towards town. One of the dockworkers followed.

"Do you know who you threw in the water?" asked the longshoreman.

"A man who cheats his workers," replied Lance.

"Yes, but that was Bulldog Warner and he's a bare-fisted fighter that's never been beat. Man, you picked him up and threw him like he was a bale of straw."

"He had it coming."

"He sure did. Say, did you ever think of fighting? You could earn some real money at it."

"I am in need of food and some place to find clothes."

"Folks 'round here call me Fast Eddy. I'll show you a place to eat and then a used clothing store. Maybe they'll have a few pieces that would fit someone like you."

"I'll be needing shoes the most."

Lance held up an old boot and the heels were worn down and the sole cracked in half.

"I don't know, you're sort of a king-sized feller."

Lance could smell food and he began to follow his nose through twisted streets.

"That's the place," said Fast Eddy.

The two men went in the restaurant and sat down. There were several booths and a long counter. Men crowded the little eatery and the smell of cooking onions was strong. Fast Eddy ordered coffee and Lance ordered liver and

25

onions, mashed potatoes, beans and coffee. It didn't take long for the food to arrive and while eating, conversation was impossible. The new acquaintance watched the big man put away everything on his plate. Lance finished, but declared he was still hungry and ordered two pieces of apple pie. On his third cup of coffee, he asked where the clothing shop was.

It was a used clothing store and its length was three times that of its width and it was stuffed with clothing of every description. There were clothes in boxes on the floor, on wooden shelves, on hangers, and hanging above those was a second, third, and fourth tier of various attire. Dresses, pants, jackets, boots, shoes, gloves, mittens, shirts, belts, hats, hunting clothes, slickers, coats, every imaginable item made by man in the form of clothing was stuffed into that store. Lance had never seen anything like it. He was excited. He had money in his pocket and for the first time in his life he could pick out his own clothes and pay for them. In this new life of freedom, almost everything was a first.

He started with shoes and quickly learned that his enormous size made it difficult to find a pair that fit him. Finally a clerk came to help and he found boots that accommodated his large feet. The same occurred when it came to pants, shirts, and jackets. Without the clerk, Lance would never have found clothes of the proper size. There wasn't much money in his pocket and when he walked out of the store wearing a suit, he had fifty cents remaining.

"You look like a new man," said Fast Eddy, noting the passersby stopping to observe the well-dressed giant.

"I need to find a job and a place to stay," said Lance.

"You can board with me," replied Fast Eddy. "I got a cot—perhaps—ahh—you could sleep on a pallet on the floor. You can work the docks during the week and every Saturday night there are the bare-knuckle fights. Between the two you should do very well."

"What about the dock foreman I threw in the water?"

"Bulldog ain't the only foreman on the docks. Just like getting a boxing match, the dock foremen will size you up and you'll be hired on the spot. And you look like a winner in that fancy suit. Suppose we drop off the work clothes at my place and then go out on the town?"

"I don't have enough money," declared Lance.

"Leave it to me," said Fast Eddy. "I know a saloon where we can get drinks on the cheap and maybe we can play a little poker."

"I don't know anything about poker," said Lance.

The apartment was little more than a room

in a square boxed building, not far from the docks. Lance left his clothes on a cot and they walked to the saloon. It was a large, high-ceilinged room with a bar along one end, and round tables and round bottom chairs. Men stood along the bar drinking beer, and the tables were surrounded by poker players and dockworkers eating pickled eggs and free sandwiches with their drinks.

Lance ordered beer and filled a plate with sand-wiches. Fast Eddy greeted men at the bar, put down coin for both, and got his own beer. He continued to say hello to friends at the tables and quickly joined a card game. After Lance finished his food, Fast Eddy called for him. As the hours passed, the day waned, and darkness took over the night. Fast Eddy introduced the young man to three vices. The first was the atmosphere of the saloon and the vigorous chatter of male insults and camaraderie around the poker table. The second vice was alcohol in the form of cheap beer, and the third was poker.

Having never experienced such social contact, at first Lance remained reticent. Then the influ-ence of alcohol, a tremendous amount indulged, began to affect him, even with his huge frame. It loosened his tongue as drink always will, and he began to partake in snappy repartee for the first time in his life. Given his enormous size, the men gave him the deference he was due. These were the very same men who had seen the young man fling Bulldog, the foreman, off the dock as if he were a ragdoll.

"You weasel!" raved Lance. "Deal me a good hand or I'll bruise your liver!"

Fast Eddy stared at his new friend with admiration and a bit of fear. By his own count the young man had drunk fifteen beers and yet he was still able to sit, talk, and play poker. Another man, including himself, would be under the table with that amount of alcohol consumed. Lance claimed he had never played poker in his life, but within a couple hours the young man seemed to absorb and comprehend the nine different possible hands a player can hold, from a royal flush, down to a single high card.

"This game's kind of fun," exclaimed Lance, pulling in another hand of pennies, nickels, dimes, and quarters.

"Lance," said one of the card players. "If you never played before, how come you're winning so darned much?"

"Why this game's simple, once a feller figures out what it takes to win."

"Tell us what that is?" asked one of the dock-workers, sitting at the table.

"You boys know it's just not what a feller's holding, but how he plays 'em," replied Lance, and then he winked as he swayed slightly from

29

the effects of alcohol. "Bartender! Buy everyone in the joint a beer!"

"Lance!" exclaimed Fast Eddy. "You're spending all your winnings. You'll need some of that for food and rent."

"No problem," replied Lance. "I'll just win a few more hands and then we'll go. The smoke in this joint is killing me."

Lance was right. Between cigarettes, pipes, cigars, and emissions from the burning lanterns, the air was blue with drifting smoke.

"Thank God for the bad air," said Fast Eddy. "I thought you were going to stay all night. We have to get up and go to work tomorrow."

Lance was coughing, his lungs reacting to the smoky assault they received. They went back to the apartment and he was asleep the second he stretched out on the blanketed floor.

In the morning they awoke and had boiled eggs and coffee and were at the docks at the crack of dawn. Fast Eddy kept looking but could see no effects of the night before on his large friend. The big young man did not seem to suffer from the alcohol or the limited sleep. As Fast Eddy predicted, Lance was hired on the spot and all day long the two labored with other dockworkers to load and unload the large steam packets that came to port.

They worked the remainder of the week and

on Saturday they quit at four. They cleaned up in their rented room and went to a restaurant for supper.

"How do you feel?" asked Fast Eddy.

"I'm not tired, if that's what you mean," said Lance.

"At six, I'll take you to the docks and introduce you to Miss Lilly and Big Mississippi."

"Who are they?"

"They run the fights around here and plenty of other deals. You don't get to fight unless they say so."

"How much will I get for a fight?" asked Lance.

"You box for free and ten dollars if you win against all comers. Since I'm your manager, I'm in for ten percent."

"Ten percent?"

"Yeah, since I'm setting this up, I get ten percent of what you earn," said Fast Eddy.

"I'm doing the fighting. Why should you get anything?"

"I'm not cheating you," protested Eddy. "Managers always get ten percent. That's how it works."

At six they walked toward the docks and before they came to the water there were several warehouses. They stopped before two large buildings which created a long narrow space and men were gathered smoking and talking. There was a table set up, and an attractive woman sat behind it, collecting a twenty-five cent admission fee and taking bets on the main event which was advertised on a poster.

"Miss Lilly," began Fast Eddy, laying down fifty cents. "Meet Lance. He would like to fight in the open bare-knuckle event."

Miss Lilly looked up, caught one glance of the giant and rose to her feet. Smiling, she put out a hand for the tall young man to shake.

"Well," said Miss Lilly, "it's been a long time since Fast Eddy has brought such a specimen as you . . ."

"Spe-ci-men?" asked Lance.

"Fighter," explained Miss Lilly. "You are a fighter?"

"I've been in fights all my life," replied Lance. "I've used my fist but mostly I'm a wrestler."

"There's no wrestling allowed," said Miss Lilly. "Fists only, known as bare knuckle and skull. Fast Eddy, you didn't bring a wrestler to a boxing match?"

"Maybe I did," replied Eddy. "But I guarantee you he won't have any trouble defending himself. Meet the feller who threw Bulldog Warner off the docks."

"So!" exclaimed Lilly, her eyes lighting up. "Fast Eddy, take him over to Big Mississippi and tell him what you told me. Lance gets the first fight on the dock. If he's that good, he ought to beat all comers and win the purse."

"What about next week?" asked Eddy.

"You know the answer to that. He has to build a reputation before he can get a big fight."

Fast Eddy took Lance to a crowd of men. The biggest of them was a man dressed in a black suit and wearing a wide-brimmed hat. He was six feet tall, and with huge chest, arms, and legs, and even a larger belly. He stood talking in a booming voice. The men stopped to eye the newcomer, and Fast Eddy introduced Lance to Big Mississippi.

"Seldom I meet a man bigger than me," said the promoter. "Can you fight, boy?"

"I'm not your boy," replied Lance.

The big-bellied man grinned, showing large coffee-stained teeth, and put out a hand to shake. Lance stared at it, and both knew what would come next. The younger man spread his feet for balance and then extended his right. The two grasped hands and Big Mississippi did not release his grip but instead increased it. Face to face, Lance towered three inches over the larger and older man with the wide girth. They stood toe-to-toe in a hand squeezing contest. Fast Eddy and the crowd of men took immediate interest and as seconds passed, the hand crushing continued. The men began to cheer for their man of choice. The majority took the side of Big Mississippi. Fast Eddy and a few others sided with Lance.

"Crush him!" called the men.

"Get him, Mississippi!"

"You can beat him, Lance!" called Fast Eddy.

As the grips of the two adversaries increased, the men began to see sweat start to drip from the face of the fight promoter. There appeared to be no indication of pain on the younger man's visage. Then Big Mississippi cried out.

"Stop!"

Lance immediately lessened his grip and the two big men released their clenched hands.

"Big Mississippi," said Fast Eddy, grinning ear to ear. "Meet the lad that threw Bulldog Warner off the dock."

"I was wondering when you would come around," said Big Mississippi. "I see the story wasn't exaggerated. First time I've ever been beat. What did Miss Lilly say?"

"She said Lance would take the first fight in the open bare-knuckle."

"Right," said Big Mississippi. "At least now I know which way to bet. Get your man ready, we start right at seven."

The boxing match was a crude affair where two fighters were surrounded by spectators as they fought bare-knuckle, no rounds, no time out, to the end. Lance was introduced and men cheered. His opponent was a dockworker with the nickname Fire Jack. Jack was a solid barrel of a man with massive arms and bulging biceps. He was bald and a foot shorter than Lance. But then, most men were. Jack came at Lance and threw a quick series of punches, one which made solid contact with Lance's chin, before the big man stepped back.

"Put up your fists!" yelled Fast Eddy. "Protect yourself!"

Lance ignored the advice and Fire Jack came at Lance once again with a series of lefts and rights. The smaller fighter got inside Lance's waving arms and open hands and made a series of thumping blows to the big man's body. Then Lance doubled up a right hand and in a windmill motion circled his arm and the big fist came down onto the top of Fire Jack's head. He fell unconscious as if struck with a sledgehammer.

Members of the crowd cheered or booed depending on which way their bets went. Fast Eddy rushed in and pulled Lance from the crowd.

"How did I do?" asked Lance, grinning widely.

"You don't know a thing about boxing, do you?"

"No."

"First off, keep your fists clenched and at face level. That will protect you. You punch with fists and you try for the chin, not the top of the head."

"I knocked him out, didn't I?"

"Yes, but this is a boxing match, not a free-for-all. The men will call foul and want their bets back. You watch the next fight and see how it's done and then copy the winner."

Lance did as Eddy instructed and he was a keen

observer. The two men fighting were of equal height and weight. One had his shirt off and exposed rippling muscles, a tight gut, and huge biceps. The other man seemed flabbier and with a bulging belly. The two exchanged punches to the face and to the body, and the muscular man seemed faster. Lance watched each fighter take a boxing stance, left foot forward, right foot behind, both hands clenched, elbows bent, left fist leading, followed by the right. He watched the rhythm of it, and one man punched three times with a left and then followed it with a hooking right.

It was not only the fighting that Lance noticed but the enthusiasm of the crowd. He saw Miss Lilly, her face flushed with excitement. Her appearance was distorted with the brutal desire to see mayhem. This made the lines of her face change and she was no longer beautiful, but now appeared twisted and ugly. Looking at other visages in the crowd, Lance saw similar bloodthirsty grimaces. He came to a sudden realization that these people did not care about the boxers at all. They wanted to see both men destroy each other and if it was not for the betting, they would not even favor one boxer over the other.

As soon as I win a little money, I'll quit this game, thought Lance. *I have no liking to pound or hurt any man just for money.*

Lance went back to watching the fighters. The two men threw punches and many were blocked by the left forearm and then the opponent would throw a wicked right. The muscular man threw a right fist and it made contact with the other boxer's flabby belly. The slower fighter stepped back and threw a right of his own and the muscular man was struck squarely in the chin and he went down, out cold. Lance could see it was not always the strongest who won a fight, but who placed the best blow.

The next fight was between Lance and a fellow named Iron George. This man took off his shirt and exposed rippling muscles. The fight was announced by Big Mississippi and he shouted out the name *Windmill Lance* as the opponent. Lance stepped out, surrounded by shouting voices and a ring of excited men. The other boxer threw a bare left, once, twice, three times, and Lance stepped back; one blow struck air, another his left fist, and the third touched his chin. Then Iron George stepped in and followed with a right and Lance parried it with his left arm and struck hard with his right into the other man's chin. The smack of the punch resounded loudly above the shouting voices and Iron George fell backwards, hitting the ground hard. The fight was over before it had barely started. The crowd booed in unison.

"You learn real fast," shouted Fast Eddy,

smiling ear to ear. "Never seen it done more perfect."

There were two more open fights scheduled before the main event, with Lance taking on the winner. Lance stood above everyone in the crowd when Big Mississippi approached him, a sour grimace upon the fight promoter's face.

"I'd say you finished that fight off too quick. You made it look easy. One fight you appeared liked a wrestler who didn't know what he was doing and the second fight, like a professional. Anyway, after seeing you work, the other four men quit. You win the purse tonight."

Big Mississippi handed Lance a ten-dollar coin.

"What happens next Saturday?" asked Lance.

"I'll have to see who we can line up to fight. The way it looks, no one wants to challenge you. Perhaps Bulldog Warner will take you on next week. He's in the big fight tonight and has been undefeated for a year."

"The purse is fifty dollars!" exclaimed Fast Eddy.

"If he wants it, I'll stand against him," said Lance.

"Warner said you hit him when he wasn't lookin'," said Big Mississippi. "He says he's looking forward to giving you a good cleaning."

"I saw Lance throw that lying foreman in the drink, and there was no trickery about it," said Eddy.

38

"Yeah," said Big Mississippi. "You fight Bulldog Warner next Saturday. That ought to bring in a crowd. We'll print up posters early and charge fifty cents instead of twenty-five. That way, the other boxers won't be afraid to fight in the open bare-knuckle event before the big fight."

"When do you want me here?" asked Lance.

"Come at six," replied Big Mississippi, grinning and flashing his large yellow teeth. "Give a chance for Bulldog and the crowd to get a look at you before the big fight. Might increase the betting."

Lance and Fast Eddy stayed to watch Bulldog Warner knock out his opponent after a ten-minute match. It was evident to the crowd that Warner was milking it, and had the man beat after the first three minutes. When the crowd began to boo loudly, Warner cruelly beat his lesser opponent to a pulp. Bulldog hit the defenseless man squarely in the nose, breaking it, and knocking him out.

"I hope you do the same to him," said Fast Eddy. "That skunk has had it coming for a long time."

Lance and Fast Eddy worked the next week, putting in long hours and getting paid on Saturday. Posters were placed all around the docks and through the town, announcing the fight between Bulldog Warner and Windmill

Lance. Many of the men had come up to Lance and thumped him on the back, saying they were looking forward to the fight and they hoped that he would teach Warner a lesson.

"I told ya, everybody hates Bulldog," said Fast Eddy.

The two had cleaned up and then taken a light supper at a little eatery on the docks. At six, they appeared at the warehouse and Fast Eddy paid the dollar entrance fee. Miss Lilly was at her table and when she saw Lance, she was all smiles. Again she stood up and shook his hand.

"After the fight," said Miss Lilly. "Will you come and speak to me?"

"What about?" asked Fast Eddy.

"You're not invited," said Miss Lilly. "Besides, I wasn't talking to you."

"You want to speak to me?" asked Lance. "Fast Eddy's my manager; if it's about fighting, he's in on it too."

"Well, if you must, bring him," responded Lilly. "Better we meet in the little office. Fast Eddy knows where it is."

Lance and his manager walked into a large crowd, and many of the men came forward to greet the big man and thump him on the back.

"Step away, fellows!" shouted Fast Eddy. "Give the man a break, he has to fight tonight. He don't need no pounding before it."

The crowd of men did step back. Among them

were a few women accompanied by men in suits. This was rare for the docks and Fast Eddy said so.

"Did you make a bet on yourself?" Fast Eddy asked Lance.

"No. Here's ten dollars. I thought you would do it for me and know who to trust."

"I do," said Fast Eddy. "And I'm not going near Miss Lilly or Big Mississippi. They're crooks, if you haven't figured it out by now. You hold on, and I'll be right back."

There was a large crowd on the dock, and Lance watched his manager push through it to go make his bet. The odds were fifty/fifty, an even match. No one would be making much unless they bet big. Lance found a bunch of boxes next to one of the warehouses and he sat down. There were butterflies in his stomach, and he wondered if he could really beat Warner. When he grabbed hold of him on the docks and threw him in the water, he gave the man no chance to fight. This time it would be different, and the dock foreman was a proven boxer.

Can I avoid those fists? thought Lance. *This time I can't just pick him up and throw him.*

Fast Eddy returned and found another box and sat down. The manager's expression was grim and he looked worried too.

"You look like I already lost the fight," said Lance.

"No," replied Fast Eddy. "It's just that I never bet all my money on a fight before."

"You're having second thoughts," said Lance. "You're worried about those big fists of Warner's and his skill at bare-knuckle."

Fast Eddy looked up at his friend in wonder.

"You got brains," he said, smiling genuinely for the first time in hours. "I feel better already. Yeah, I admit, I'm worried about that, but seeing that you know it, makes me feel better. I'm removing my doubts; you just watch that right of his, and stand back. When you get the chance, you break that face of his in two."

Both men sat against the warehouse and listened to the open bare-knuckle fights. With Lance out of the picture there were six fights and the last one took more than twenty-five minutes. They were late starting the big event.

"Ladies and Gentlemen!" announced Big Mississippi in his booming voice. "All bets are in! The odds are fifty/fifty. First we have the undefeated bare knuckle champion of the docks, Bulldog Warner!"

Most of the crowd booed. There were very few cheers.

"Now . . . from parts unknown . . . the new-comer everyone has been talking about . . . Big Windmill Lance!"

Nearly everyone in the crowd cheered. Some-one shoved Lance from behind and he went into the center of the ring, and just as Big Mississippi was about to speak, Bulldog Warner pushed him aside and struck Lance a hard right to the cheek. This sent Lance reeling backward, the crowd jeered loudly, and Big Mississippi sidestepped and backed away. Bulldog raced forward to strike Lance twice more in the head. Lance fell backward into the crowd and men held him up while Bulldog pounded fists into the big man's stomach.

Forgetting the rules, Lance regained his feet, reached out with two long arms, grabbed hold of Bulldog Warner and picked him up and threw him into the center of the ring. The man fell and rolled.

"Not fair!" yelled men in the crowd.

"Foul!" yelled several others.

Big Mississippi ran into the center of the ring.

"All right! All right! Bulldog struck before I said begin! Lance was being held by the crowd and defending himself. Now let's start over and make this a fair fight!"

The crowd cheered, and Lance, shaking his head, stood at the edge of the circle waiting for his vision to clear. Warner came to his knees, then to his feet, also shaken from being thrown. Both men stared wickedly at each other, and the crowd noise increased into a roar as the two fighters clenched fists, ready to box.

Bulldog stepped forward and threw a quick

left. It struck Lance's left fist. Bulldog kept advancing, sidestepping and throwing lefts, while Lance continued to back up. He came against the crowd and men shoved. Bulldog Warner took advantage and threw a quick series of lefts and then a right which struck hard on Lance's chin. Sliding away from the crowd and their grasping hands, Lance got to the middle of the ring, where he was determined to stay. There were cheaters in that crowd who were out to get him.

Bulldog circled and then advanced. The more experienced boxer, he kept coming, throwing repeated lefts and making Lance back up. Remembering hands that shoved or held him, Lance stayed away from the crowd and circled in the middle of the ring. Each time Bulldog moved forward, throwing lefts and waiting for the moment to throw a right. Lance, the taller man by several inches, had the advantage of height and reach. It was debatable who had the greater strength. Bulldog was a mass of muscle and the bare-chested man sported an ugly growth of hair. Lance hated making contact with the man's sweaty hairy chest and arms.

Bulldog Warner stepped in, threw three quick punches and a quick right that struck hard on Lance's chin. The big man tasted blood, and he threw a series of rights and lefts of his own. Both boxers stood toe-to-toe throwing punches and the crowd roared. It was Lance who threw a ringing right to Bulldog's head that stopped the frenzy of punches, and Warner stepped back. This time Lance advanced, the pain in his jaw and the series of blows making his head ring. Anger took away caution and pain, and Lance threw a left and right at his opponent with all the strength he could muster. Blows were returned and again the men were toe-to-toe, throwing lefts and rights. This time both fighters took the punishment for as long as they could, and then backed up. The crowd screamed encouragement.

His head ringing with pain, his chest and belly feeling as if struck with hammers, Lance advanced first and struck a left and a right at Bulldog. The man was still trying to recover from the series of blows he received and was awkward at defending himself. Lance struck him hard on the chin, and Bulldog fell to one knee. The crowd roared louder than before, and thoroughly deaf, Lance stepped forward. When Bulldog stood up, he was struck with a right that dazed him. Taking advantage, Lance moved closer and planting his feet he began to throw fists to the stomach, chest, face, and chin of the other man. The blows rocked Bulldog Warner on his feet. The crowd was a constant roar now, and with his head beginning to clear, Lance struck with all his strength. Still the man did not go down. It was as if he were made of stone.

Bulldog dropped his arms and Lance advanced,

striking a blow to the gut, to the side of his face, and then to his chin. The hairy monster of a man, blood dripping from mouth and nose, jerked back several steps, barely keeping his balance. To the roar of the crowd, Lance stepped forward and remembering last Saturday night's fight, planted a right into the middle of Bulldog Warner's face. The smack of the punch sounded loud even in the crowd noise. The big man's nose poured a fountain of blood and was clearly slanted sideways. Bulldog Warner, nearly out on his feet, still remained standing. Lance stepped in and threw one final right up under the bully's chin. The hairy man slammed backwards onto the hard ground and did not move.

The crowd went quiet for a few seconds, and then Big Mississippi appeared and raised Lance's right arm.

"The winner!" shouted the fight promoter.

The crowd cheered and then Fast Eddy came up to Lance and grabbed hold of his bruised and bleeding partner.

"Come with me," said Eddy. "I got a bucket and a towel to clean you up with."

Lance, with Fast Eddy's help, worked his way through the crowd toward the warehouse with the boxes. Men slapped Lance heavily on the back, and despite Fast Eddy's protest or effort to protect the fighter, many of the blows could not be stopped. At the boxes, Lance sat down and

Fast Eddy was there with a wet towel, gently wiping blood from several cuts and from a dripping nose.

"You beat him!" said Fast Eddy, in praise.

"It was harder than I thought," replied Lance. "He's made of rock. A couple times he nearly got me."

"Here's the towel," said Fast Eddy. "I'll hold the bucket and you clean yourself up."

The crowd began to disperse. Many more of the dockworkers came forward and called to Lance and congratulated him for winning the fight and filling their bets. Fast Eddy had gone off to collect on their bets and he came back smiling. Eventually the night quieted and Lance finished using the towel. The bleeding had stopped. His face felt swollen and sore, but the aches and pains to head and body diminished.

"That was sure some fight," said Fast Eddy. "Here's your twenty from your ten-dollar bet. Now we go collect the fifty-dollar purse and we can go home."

"Where's their office?" asked Lance. "Remember, Miss Lilly said she wanted to talk to us."

"Maybe we should leave collecting the purse for another time," said Fast Eddy. "I don't like this. Everybody's gone and there's only you and me. Who knows how many men Big Mississippi and Miss Lilly got."

"Do you think they'll try something?"

"I wouldn't trust neither one of those birds," replied Fast Eddy.

"I'm not leaving without that fifty," said Lance.

"Suit yourself, but don't tell me I didn't warn you. You've already had one fight tonight."

Fast Eddy led the way. They walked in the dark past the two warehouses and to a little building in the back. It was lit up inside and out and there were several tough-looking men standing around. Fast Eddy counted five.

"I don't like this," repeated the manager.

They came to the door of the little building and it opened. Miss Lilly came out first, followed by Big Mississippi.

"Good fight," said Big Mississippi, in his booming voice.

Miss Lilly stood smiling. She was wearing a blue dress that accentuated her figure. In the light of the lantern her yellow hair gleamed and she looked quite pretty. Except during the fights, she was one of those beauties who normally showed little facial expression, as if her countenance was made of ivory.

"I came for my purse," said Lance.

"Before we get to that," said Big Mississippi, "there's something we need to discuss."

"What's that?" asked Lance, grimacing, and then wincing at the pull of a cut on his lip.

"I want you to fight for me. There's big money in it, but not here. You played out all the fighters round here. Your next fight should be along the river. We can go from town to town and build up a reputation. Then we can hit St. Louis and we can demand a larger purse. You should earn big money, get rich . . ."

"You mean, you would get rich," interjected Lance.

"Both of us," replied Big Mississippi.

"What about Fast Eddy?" asked Lance. "He's my . . ."

"He's out," said Big Mississippi.

"I don't think so," said Lance.

"You don't think what?" asked Big Mississippi. "That Fast Eddy is out, or that you won't box for me?"

"Both," replied Lance.

"He doesn't understand," said Miss Lilly. "You explain it to him."

"You're green, boy," said Big Mississippi. "Too green to know that you should be afraid. Let me help you understand. See those men out there? Those five are armed, and within my voice are another ten. And all up and down this dock I have men that owe me. You see, there isn't one shipment that goes in or out of this city that I don't have a hand in and I don't get a cut of. I got men working for me all up and down this river and there isn't one place in Missouri you can run that I won't find out about it. Now, *boy,* do you understand?"

"I told you," replied Lance. "I'm not your boy."

There was a long silence and then Big Mississippi laughed. Miss Lilly joined in.

"You've got guts," said Big Mississippi. "I'll give you that."

"Some time back I vowed that I would rather be dead then to let another man have control over me, or make me their slave."

"Like I been explaining, that can be arranged," replied Big Mississippi.

"Lance," began Miss Lilly. "What's the problem? You're just doing what comes naturally. You're a born fighter. Why not fight for us and become rich at it? Fight for us and you can have anything your heart desires."

"I made up my mind," said Lance. "Tonight . . . was my last fight."

"Don't talk crazy," said Miss Lilly, coming closer and putting her two hands on Lance's arm. "If you come with us, you and I might even become close friends."

"I won't fight and I won't work for either of you," replied Lance.

Fast Eddy, standing next to Lance, groaned audibly and in real fear.

"You'll fight for us, or die!" shouted Big Mississippi, pulling a small pistol from a wide sash at his middle.

The five men moved closer and gleaming steel

could be seen in their hands. Again Fast Eddy groaned.

"I won't let another man make me a slave!" shouted Lance and in a white-hot heat he launched himself at the three-hundred-pound giant.

The big man roared as Lance put his two large, powerful hands around Mississippi's throat. The force of the attack shoved Big Mississippi back and together they fell to the ground against the shack. At the same time the pistol discharged and the bullet struck one of the five men in the side and passed through him and into a second man. There was a large anvil that had been sitting against the outside wall for many years—a heavy piece of iron someone had placed there for decoration, or perhaps because it was too heavy to move. It was the edge of the anvil that Big Mississippi's head struck. His skull caved in as if made of plaster. He was dead the moment his body collapsed onto the ground.

Three of the men still standing advanced towards Lance. One had a pistol and two had knives. Fast Eddy, eying a large hammer that lay on a table near the door, ran to it. Picking it up, he threw it at the man with the pistol. It struck his head and as he fell, the weapon discharged into the back of one of the men holding a knife. The last guard standing was now confronted by Lance who had risen to his feet. This enforcer took one look at the giant, turned, and ran.

"You killed him!" cried Miss Lilly. "You killed Big Mississippi!"

"He was going to kill me," replied Lance in a remarkably steady voice. "I want my purse money."

"Never!" exclaimed Miss Lilly. "Not if you were the last man on earth!"

"I won it, I need it, and I'm going to get it," said Lance, in as calm a voice as Fast Eddy had ever heard.

All along the docks men were shouting.

"Help! Help!" yelled the guard who had run away. "Miss Lilly needs help!"

"Come on, Lance!" said Fast Eddy. "We got to get out of here!"

"Not until I get my money," said Lance.

The tall giant grabbed Lilly's left hand and squeezed. She reached for something in her clothing with her right hand, and when a tiny single-shot derringer appeared, Lance knocked it away.

"You're hurting me!" said Miss Lilly.

"Give me my fifty dollars," said Lance, squeezing harder.

"Here," she said, producing a small pull string purse. "There's more than fifty in there."

Lance took the soft pouch, opened it and poured three twenty dollar coins into his hand.

He kept the three coins and then reached in his pocket and pulled out a ten-dollar gold piece. He added it to her silk reticule and then flung it before Miss Lilly's feet.

"I took what was mine," said Lance. "I'm no thief."

"That won't save you!" she replied bitterly and then began to shout. "Help! Help! Murder!"

"Follow me!" exclaimed Fast Eddy.

Lance stepped over several of the fallen men and broke into a run as he raced behind Eddy. They sprinted towards the docks and the river. As they ran, a group with guns suddenly appeared before them. Big Mississippi had not lied. Many of the longshoremen worked for him. Fast Eddy turned to the right along the wharf. He came to a large dock and ran onto it. Men shouted from behind. Fast Eddy hurried forward and lapping water could be heard from below. Eddy came to a ladder and he disappeared into inky blackness. Lance followed and climbed down. They were just above the water now, and at the bottom of the ladder was a little rowboat. Eddy climbed in and began untying a rope. Lance gently stepped aboard, his vast weight making the little boat sink to its gunwales.

"Grab those oars and start rowing," whispered Eddy.

Never having rowed a boat in his life, Lance made up with strength what he lacked in skill.

The heavily laden craft began to move swiftly towards the center of the river and away from the docks.

"What now?" asked Lance.

"If you and me want to live," exclaimed Fast Eddy, "We're going to have to get off this river and go west."

"But there's Indians out there."

"I'd rather face Indians than the law, Miss Lilly, and her men."

Lance rowed the boat across the river and they landed on the opposite shore.

"Now where?" asked Lance.

"We have to find a place to buy guns and supplies. We can't go west without them."

"I don't know anything about guns."

"I don't know much myself," said Eddy. "Best we join a freight outfit or a wagon train to travel with. I have a hunch we're gonna find Californy."

"I'd like that," exclaimed Lance.

"Too bad we had to leave our things behind," said Fast Eddy. "But we're not going back to the room. They'll be watching it for sure. Good thing we kept our coin on us. I got a money belt and some savings."

"I have about seventy dollars," answered the big man.

"We should be able to buy guns, ammunition, and supplies, but we don't have enough for horses or wagons."

"We can walk."

"Men don't travel this country on foot," said Eddy, "unless it's a slow-moving wagon train, and even then they ride more than walk."

While Eddy and Lance were talking, a group of toughs, now working for Miss Lilly, touched the shore in two large rowboats. They pulled the boats up near the small skiff the escapees had used.

"I heard something," whispered Lance.

He turned and saw the thugs getting off the boats.

"They've followed us," answered Fast Eddy. "Miss Lilly probably offered a reward for our hides. A big one, I venture."

Lance left the shore and ran for the cover of small trees and brush. The two crashed through the vegetation, making a terrific noise as it grabbed and tore at their clothing.

"Let's run west, and then head north," said Fast Eddy. "They'll think we went south towards St. Louis."

Lance led the way, and in the dark they stumbled over stones and vines. They must have been heard, because there came shouting voices from behind them.

"They've got guns and knives," said Fast Eddy. "All we got is the clothes on our back."

As quickly as they could, the two traveled north, following the course of the river. In the dark they would be hard to find and there was no possible way the hunting party could trail them. It wasn't long and the noise of the pursuers stopped. Lance whispered to Fast Eddy.

"What do you think will happen?"

"Those men won't give up. They'll find our tracks in the morning and follow."

"Then we have to hide, or find a different way to travel."

"It's worse than that," explained Fast Eddy. "Miss Lilly will make up some story how you killed Big Mississippi. She'll call in the law, offer a reward, and posters will be put up. They'll probably do the same with me. All up and down the river and all through Missouri we'll be wanted men. We've got to go west and stay there."

CHAPTER FOUR

Katy sat on the wagon seat and beside her, snuggled close, was her son Johnny. Using both hands she held the long leather reins controlling the four mules. It was second nature to her now. For months she sat on the blanketed seat, bouncing along the worn trail, doing her best to avoid the deep ruts. Tanned by the sun, her face felt stiff and windburned. She hated having to use axle grease for her complexion; it was just one more hardship she endured.

Her father was on his horse, riding ahead as he often did. Today he went hunting and said he would return with venison. Ever since leaving Illinois, her father had pushed, always anxious to reach the California gold fields as soon as possible. They had not rested, not once. The animals were thoroughly worn out. So much so that the mules were losing their strength and pulling less each day.

Many times Peter Day's enthusiasm put them in danger. During a raging rainstorm near Fort Laramie, he forced the four wagons across the South Platte, and it was Katy's wagon that went last, with her son aboard. With each passing moment the river rose and began to turn into a raging rush of water. The torrent lifted the heavy wagon up off its wheels and it began to float sideways, dragging the mules with it. It happened that two of the party thought to use caution and be prepared. If it hadn't been for ropes and the quick thinking of her Uncle Clare and Frank Sparks, they would have disappeared in the rising flood.

When on firm ground, in the pouring rain, Katy angrily confronted her father.

"You nearly killed my son! You keep taking risks, you keep pushing us! We're exhausted, the animals are worn out. Look at them! Nearly skin and bone. Johnny and I aren't going any further until we rest."

"I'm the leader of this party, and you'll do as I say, daughter," replied Peter Day.

"That may be so, but I'm firm on this. You said Fort Laramie is near. When we reach it, we stop and stay as long as it takes. Long enough to buy proper supplies and rest our bodies and the mules. Weeks—if necessary."

"You won't be dictating to me!"

"Father! The mules are so weak they're stumbling. We're so worn out, we can hardly walk. We're stopping and resting for as long as it takes for us to recover."

"That's my wagon you're riding on; it's my money that's paying for this trip; you'll do as I say!"

Standing near the wagon now, were her uncles,

Clare and Harold Day. Joe and Frank Sparks had left their conveyance to hear what the delay was about. The rain poured down and except for Johnny, who was under canvas, her father, Katy, and the other men were drenched.

"She has a point," said Clare. "I was going to say the same thing. We should stop and rest these poor beasts."

"It would be foolish to push these mules any further until they've rested and fattened up," added Harold.

"Are all of you against me?" bellowed Peter. "Who's leading this party anyway?"

"You are," said Joe Sparks. "But all of us need a rest and supplies. Fort Laramie will be the place to stop."

"I have a mind to take my wagon and money and head out on my own."

"Fine," replied Katy, forever losing fear of her unreasonable parent. "Be a stubborn old fool."

Angrily her father dismounted and stepped up on the wagon and raised a hand to strike his daughter. Uncle Clare admonished him.

"You hit that woman and I'll strike you, Peter. You forget yourself. Now climb back on your horse and lead us to the fort. Enough is enough, brother."

Hand still raised in anger, Peter slowly lowered it. Everyone in the party looked tired, thin of face, and strained.

"I suppose stopping would not be a bad thing," said Peter Day. "But daughter, I won't never forget this here thing you done."

The angry man climbed down off the wagon, and in the fierce downpour mounted his horse. The others went back to their vehicles. Shortly, through wet mud, the tired mules began to slowly pull their loads up the California Trail.

Red Jennings reined his team forward, following the mule and the mounted old man who was guiding the party of eight wagons. Horntoad Harry had kept up an even pace since leaving Fort Kearny. Now they were traveling slower than they ever had. Other wagon trains and groups of mounted men leading pack mules passed them daily. The members of the St. Louis Gold Association complained. The old frontiersman had them stop early in the evening to graze and rest the mules. Then he insisted on having tied ropes between the circled wagons and placing the mules inside the makeshift corral. All this took time and seemed to delay them further.

One evening before dark, and around the cook fire, a heated argument began among the men, Red Jennings, and the frontiersman.

"We're moving too slow," complained Hezekiah. "How come we got to listen to that old man all the time?"

"Yeah," agreed Jake. "There's prospectors

passing us all day, every day, and I'm sick of it."

The other men murmured agreement. The air was thick with their anger.

"I'm tired of all this caution about no fires at night, not crossing a stream when it rains, making camp early, and all the extra work of grazing and corralling the stock," complained Zeke. "Ain't no one else movin' this slow."

"We voted to hire the frontiersman to lead us," said Red. "We haven't lost any animals and not one of us has suffered from an accident. You saw those wagons and teams swept away in that flooded river. Horntoad made us wait it out. How many others did we watch cross too soon and lose stock and supplies?"

There was a long silence and one of the men threw a chunk of wood into the cook fire. The wood was wet and smoke billowed up.

"That's what I'm talkin' about!" shouted Horntoad angrily. "Wet wood on a fire! A green-horn stunt like that on this open plain and you're invitin' to be attacked."

"How come you always got some fool order, old man?" asked Zeke. "You don't know everything!"

"I know a heap more than you do about these plains," replied the old-timer. "Bet you didn't realize we're reaching towards the heart of Sioux and Cheyenne country. A fool stunt, a wrong move, a bad decision and every one of you could have your scalp hangin' in some warrior's lodge."

"Aww, you're just trying to scare us, old man," said one of the seventeen crowding round the fire.

"This ain't no race!" replied Horntoad, loud enough for each man to hear. "I promised to git you to Californy with your hair on. Tarnation, I helped blaze part of this trail. I lived out here all my life and I knows what's what. Fire me if you like, but you fellers follow my lead, or I leave."

"The men are upset," defended Red. "They don't understand you being so cautious and moving so slow."

"Dang it! Any fool can understand this!" growled Horntoad. "When others have their mules stolen in the middle of the night, ours will be safe behind this here corral. When others push their stock and themselves to the limit, we'll be as fresh and strong as the day we left Fort Kearny. When folks up and get sick from typhoid, cholera, scurvy, bad food, and water, we'll still be healthy. There's Injuns, more rivers, quicksand, fever, storms, thieves, killers, every kind of danger facing us for the next two thousand miles. If you think you can do better than me, then . . ."

"For an old man you sure brag," said someone from the back of the group.

The old man jumped to his feet. He turned his back and headed for his saddle and gear.

"See who the fool is when you push your animals to death and you don't have no way of going forward or back!" shouted the angry plainsman.

Picking up a rope from gear set under a wagon, Horntoad stepped into a circle of animals and threw a loop around his sturdy Missouri mule. Tying the line to a wagon wheel, he began to blanket and saddle the animal.

"Men!" shouted Red. "I vote we still follow Horntoad. Those that agree come and stand beside me."

One of the group came forward immediately and stood beside Red. Slowly, one at a time, others came forward. Zeke, Jake, and Hezekiah remained in the background. Finally, they too reluctantly moved towards the party of men.

"Good!" said Red. "Then it's settled, we'll follow what Horntoad tells us."

The plainsman lifted saddlebags and placed them over the rear of the mule and began to tie them down.

"Horntoad, we want you to guide us to California," Red told the frontiersman.

The old-timer continued tying and did not respond.

"It doesn't mean some of us won't complain at your orders from time to time, being what we are, but we'd be obliged if you would stay," continued Red.

"I'll let no man bad-mouth me," replied Horntoad.

"Whoever spoke was just blowing off steam," explained Red. "We're all anxious to get to California. Being together like we are, traveling all day over this endless prairie, wears on a man. Horntoad, you know we need you."

"You betcha!" said the old-timer, turning and facing the group. "Now suppose you prove it." He leered and then held up a right hand and rubbed thumb and fingers together. Some of the men groaned.

"He's holding us up for more money," complained Jake Vargas, the second leader of the Gold Association.

"What did you expect?" shouted Red. "We insulted the man and now we're begging him to stay."

"What's it going to be?" asked Horntoad, standing firm, one hand on buckskinned hip and the other on the handle of a wide Bowie knife.

"Would you take another hundred dollars?" asked Red.

"Done!" replied Horntoad. "Now, how about if one of you dish me up a plate and bring it over to that wagon tongue. I'm hungry, and I'm eatin' alone tonight."

CHAPTER FIVE

Lance and Fast Eddy walked all night and when first light began to spread across the land, they came upon an odd construction. It was a crudely made building, part adobe, part boards and cut poles. The roof slanted crookedly, round limbs stuck out beneath a covering of buffalo hides. At one time dried adobe mud layered the roof. Rain had eaten through much of this mud, and the large hides were exposed, hairy side up.

"What kind of place is this?" asked Fast Eddy.

"You two make enough noise for a herd of buffalo," said a bearded, long-haired old man, wearing a fur hat and holding a brand-new Sharps. "I heard you two coming for a quarter of a mile."

"We don't want any trouble, mister," said Fast Eddy.

"Well, boys," said the old-timer, "you found it when you came tearing up to my cabin. Now, suppose you come a bit closer so's I can git a good look at you hombres. What's wrong with that big feller? Looks like he swallowed too many watermelons and grew twice normal size."

"I don't like a man making fun of me," replied Lance.

"Think a giant like you would be used to it by now," said the old man.

"What's that awful smell?" asked Fast Eddy, coming close enough to catch the odor of the buckskinned man.

"It ain't healthy to take a bath all over until the first hot day in August. And near as I figure, it's still June."

"Mister," said Eddy, gagging from the smell. "Don't shoot, I got to back up a ways."

"This here rifle I'm holding is a brand new single-shot, percussion, breech-loading Sharps Model 1849, .44 caliber. You mess with me and I'll drill you in the head, and blow that big feller away with my Colt Dragoon. And boys, that there pistol don't care what size a man is. It'll knock down a horse, a buffalo, and two men at once. I know, 'cause I done it."

"We don't mean harm," said Lance. "We're in a hurry, and we're looking for guns and supplies."

"Being chased, are ya?" asked the old man. "Running from the law? Killed someone, did ya?"

"Mister," began Lance. "The truth is, a man tried to hold me and tell me what to do. When I said no, he drew a pistol and said he was going to kill me. I fought, and he fell and hit his head."

"There were others," exclaimed Fast Eddy. "Five men and a woman, and they tried to kill

66

us. We fought back and some of them ended up shooting each other. We ran, and . . ."

"Nine times out of ten," began the old man, "when there's a killing, there's a woman involved. I can recall . . ."

"Mister," said Lance. "Could you help us? Those men probably found our tracks by now and . . ."

"I believe I can size up a feller and get to the truth of the matter, now give me a moment to think this here thing through."

Noxious fumes were emanating from the body of the old man, and Eddy pulled a handkerchief from his pants pocket and held it up to his face. Not to rile the oldster, Fast Eddy pretended to blow his nose.

"All right, boys," began the plainsman, "for more than forty years my cohorts been calling me Horse. Now suppose you tell me your moniker."

"What's a moniker?" asked the big man.

"Your name! What you're called!"

"I only have one, it's Lance. This is my . . . err . . . this is Fast Eddy."

"I imagine you're thirsty and hungry. I got some jerky and there's water in the spring out back. You go on take a drink and I'll fetch the meat."

Behind the crude cabin the fugitives found a trickle of water flowing into a clear pond. Surrounding the pond were flowers and a large cottonwood that provided shade. The two bent and drank their fill. From a door in the back of the cabin, Horse returned with the jerky placed on a dirty plate. Eddy hesitated, but Lance hungrily took a piece and began biting and chewing with his large white teeth. Reluctantly, overcoming any squeamishness, Fast Eddy picked up a sliver of dried meat.

"Now you think I stink, Fast Eddy? Wait till you get a smell of staked buffalo hides and bloated buffs covered with flies and filled with maggots. Or dried hides on a wagon, and not bathing for a month, and covered in blood-soaked clothes."

"It sounds pretty gruesome, old man," said Eddy.

"Maybe," declared Lance, "Horse is making some kind of offer."

"That's right," said Horse. "I need two strong fellers, to help me with my trade."

"We would have to leave right now," stated Lance, "before those men from St. Louis catch up with us."

"Come on, I have a wagon, and together we'll hitch horses and ride from here. I've got all the supplies we'll need. I'll teach you two some of what I've learned. With a giant-size man, we can't help but make money and survive."

"First I want to bathe," said Lance. "Do you have soap, old man?"

"What fer? You'll end up stinkin' anyway."

"Who buys buffalo?" asked Eddy.

"It's a trade that's just startin'," replied the old man. "I sell to one of those riverboats. A dollar a green hide—and a salted tongue goes for about fifteen cents, when I can get it to 'em. Sometimes I come across them passels of folks heading west in wagon trains. They're always lookin' for fresh meat. We ain't never gonna run out of buffalo and they're free for the takin', but a miserable job it is, skinnin' them hides. I figure you two can escape those fellers, and help me at the same time."

Unnoticed, Lance had removed his shirt, boots, and pants. He walked into the pond and started splashing water around.

"Well, I'll be," said Horse. "That feller's part fish the way he takes to water."

"You could learn a lesson or two about that," said Fast Eddy.

"I told you afore, it ain't August yet, and not near hot enough. I seen many a feller take a fever and die from such foolish excess of exuberance."

"Old man," said Eddy. "Where'd you learn them big words?"

"What else is a body to do all winter long? Books, man! Books is what I got and that's how once in a while I pull up a dollar ninety-seven cent word! Haw! Haw! Haw!"

Lance came out of the water.

"That spring is cold," he exclaimed.

"I told you—" began the old man and then he got sight of the bare back of the large youth. "Lord all a mighty!"

"What?" asked Eddy, and then he too saw the pattern of healed scars, lacerations, welts, and grooves on Lance's back. "What happened to you?"

Lance had forgotten. He was hot and sweaty, and normally he would never have removed his shirt. Now it was too late.

"Never mind," replied Lance, picking up his shirt and covering the evidence of whippings he had received since childhood.

"Tarnation!" exclaimed Horse. "Never saw no white man marked up like that and still be alive."

"What do you mean, never mind?" asked Eddy. "Why Lance, whatever happened to you?"

"Now you know," replied Lance. "So let it be."

"What do you mean? Know what?"

"Can't you see?" said the old-timer. "He don't want to talk about it."

"But how . . ." persisted Eddy.

"There's only one way a feller can have a back like that," said Horse.

"I said," repeated Lance, "let it be."

"What's that?" asked Eddy.

"I remember now," said the old man. "Saw a negro man down at the court house in St. Louis that had a back like that. He was in chains and being sold."

Lance finished dressing and put on his boots. Angrily he walked away and disappeared into the woods. Eddy got up to follow and Horse called him back.

"Don't know how, but your friend's had a heap of whippings over the years. Best you let him be. I reckon a man of his size needs some time to cool off."

"Perhaps you're right," replied Fast Eddy.

"Down yonder, near the river," explained Horse, "I've got some team hosses, and some regular riding mounts. I'll go fetch 'em, hitch up the wagon, and bring it 'round front. Suppose you go in the cabin and start hauling out those sacks of food and supplies. Leave the rifles and pistols alone. I'll take care of those. By the time we go, there won't be nothin' left worth stealin'."

The old man walked away and Fast Eddy went through the door into the cabin. The smell of the place struck the younger man's senses like a wall and nearly knocked him down. The room was dark and there was no ventilation or windows. Moving quickly, Eddy found objects to block open both the front and back doors of the cluttered shack. It helped bring in light and push out the foul air. There were sacks of rice, flour, and beans; cooking utensils; blankets, and bedrolls. One thing for sure, first chance he got, he was going to wash the bedding he and Lance would be using. The last object he carried out was a wooden box of books.

The rumble of the wagon and pounding of shod hooves could be heard coming closer. Eddy went outside to meet the old man.

"You ain't got that stuff hauled out yet?"

"I'm nearly finished, except for the guns."

"Good. You start loadin' the wagon, and try to be neat about it."

"Neat?" asked Eddy incredulously, given the mess the cabin was in.

Horse took one look at his new acquaintance and laughed.

"I been thinkin' about your friend," began the old man. "A lad that grew up with them beatings must be almighty strong. I bet he's tough as nails. I'd hate to git him riled. Good thing he's on our side. I bet he's a feller to ride the river with, if you know what I mean."

"I suppose you're right again," replied Eddy. "I've seen him fight. He's mighty tough when he needs to be."

"Now you go off in the brush yonder and call his name," said Horse. "If'n you want to miss that posse, we best be movin' onto the prairie. Hard to lose wagon tracks, but I know a few tricks. 'Sides, they might not want to follow us out to Injun territory. If they jump us, I got plenty of rifles and ammunition. Every night we'll hold up on high ground. Ain't braggin' or nothing, but with a Sharps or a Hawken, I can knock down a gnat at a hundred yards."

Eddy walked in the direction he saw his friend go. It took several repeated calls before Lance appeared. He went straight to the wagon, climbed into the back, rearranged some sacks and bedding, and sprawled out. Horse carried out six rifles. Each had its own cover. He laid those on a blanket in the wagon bed. Going back in the cabin he brought out several sacks of ammunition, powder, and lead, and laid them down, along with belts and holsters, holding two more Colt Dragoons.

"Don't know if you fellers can shoot or not," said the old-timer. "But by the time the week's out, you're both gonna be crack shots, or my name ain't Horse."

The wagon pulled out with Horse at the reins and Fast Eddy by his side. Behind the wagon were tied two mustangs, tethered by rope and bridle. Two beat-up saddles rode in the wagon bed. Lance lay against the sacks, his head pillowed by odorous blankets.

"There's a trail not far off," said Horse. "We can add our wagon to the tracks and when we're far enough along, pull off on some hard ground. It'll make it tougher for anyone following us. Now tell me, boys, can either one of you carry a tune, spin a yarn, or tell a good joke?"

Suddenly Lance sat up and began to quote scripture.

"And the earth was without form, and void; and darkness was upon the face of the deep. And the Spirit of God moved upon the face of the waters."

"Genesis, chapter 1, verse 2," said Horse. "Verse 1: *In the beginning God created the heaven and the earth.*"

"I know some of it, but not all of it," declared Lance.

"I've studied on it," said Horse. "I know all the verses of creation. Verse 3: *And God said, Let there be light: and there was light.*"

"This is my favorite verse," said Lance. *"And God said, Let us make man in our image, after our likeness: and let them have dominion over the fish of the sea, and over the fowl of the air, and over the cattle, and over all the earth, and over every creeping thing that creepeth upon the earth."*

"Ahh," said Horse. "Verse 26. Now tell me, lad, how do you happen to know the Good Book so well?"

"Not so well, as I only learned my letters and a few words. But when I was little, Mammy, not my real Mammy, but the woman who raised me, would close the curtains of our shack and call for the sacred time . . ."

"What's that?" asked Eddy.

"Confound it, will you shut up and let him tell it in his own way?" growled Horse.

"Slaves were not supposed to have books or to know how to read or write. But Mammy, she was clever and she pretended not to know much, but to all of us down in the slave quarters, she taught us things, secretly, at night."

"Hold on," interrupted Fast Eddy. "You were in slave quarters?"

"For a smart feller, you sure are dumb," said Horse. "Go on, Lance."

"Those that worked in the fields were tired and all of us were hungry. Two things we always were, but somehow Mammy would have a little extra for us, some cheese and sometimes cornbread. She would gather a crowd of us: workmen, other mammys, and the children into her shack. By chimney light she would read from the Bible, a piece of it every night. And that's how's come I know a few words by chapter and verse. She also taught me how to talk proper. Of course I had to keep it secret and talk like a proper field slave around any of the white folks."

Fast Eddy was quickly learning that the smelly old man was clever, and much more than what he looked.

"That's a right fine story, Lance," said Horse. "We's mighty glad you shared it with us. Now after we git to know each other and do a little work and earn a little money, perhaps before we turn in each night, we could do some reading. I brought some mighty fine books and writers along. Fellers like Irving and Dumas and . . ."

"Could you teach me to read?" asked Lance.

"It would be my pure pleasure," replied Horse.

They rode along, bouncing over rough ground, the iron wheels rumbling, trace chains rattling, and steel shod hooves cutting and pounding into hard soil. They came to a wagon trail heading west and Horse pulled reins and turned the team onto it.

"Since we're gittin' to know one another, I'll tell you boys that I hired a couple men to go with me. That's how I happened to have all them supplies. They are gonna be some put out. But to tell you the truth, they were a couple fellers I used last year, and was plumb disappointed with. Two dumber fellers I never ran across. They could smell liquor two miles away, and I had to watch 'em. They'd rather sleep than work, drink than eat, and swear. They couldn't start or end a sentence without some cuss word crossin' their dirty mouths. I'm glad those two foul-mouthed, tobacco-chewin' fools missed the boat."

"We appreciate you taking us along with you," said Fast Eddy.

"I got a good feeling about you boys," said Horse. "How about you tellin' us, Fast Eddy, how you happened to git that name."

"Not hard to tell," said Eddy. "My Pa died

76

when I was a kid. It was me and Ma and a couple sisters. There wasn't much and I had to find ways to bring home food. When I wasn't in school, or skippin' from it, I was always running errands. I would chop wood, deliver groceries, and load wagons. I had a knack for running and hustling. Kids began to call me Fast Eddy, and the name stuck."

"How about you, Horse?" asked Eddy. "Maybe you could . . ."

"Well, boys . . . a real plainsman don't give away his thunder by tellin' much."

"After all we told you, you say something like that?" complained Fast Eddy.

"Old man's privilege. The Indians, they don't reveal nothin' less they have a reason behind it. They believe a feller that shares, gives away some of his power. Now I reckon I can tell you somethin' . . . when the time is right."

Horse stopped speaking and when the rough wagon trail took a turn to the right, he guided the horses forward and onto a patch of stones and hard ground. The flinty earth turned into a hill which the horses climbed. Hooves rang on stone, and the iron wheels grated loudly.

"Might lose any fellers followin'," commented Horse.

The team pulled the wagon to the top of the hill and on the other side and down in a deep draw was a sparkle of water. Horse reined to a stop and reached for a sheathed rifle. He pulled off the leather covering, raised a Sharps to his shoulder, and in one quick movement, aimed and fired. The report sounded loudly and then echoed. Neither Eddy nor Lance saw what the old man fired at. The oldster reloaded his rifle and set it down behind him.

"Boys," said the old man, "always keep your weapons loaded."

Grabbing the reins, Horse slapped the team across their rumps, and they headed down rocky ground. They came to a deep wash and again reins were pulled.

"Lance," said Horse, "suppose you climb down and bring up that mule deer. Six pointer, if I don't miss my guess."

By the time Lance found and dragged the deer up onto flat ground, Horse had his skinning knives out. Both younger men watched the old man cut the neck and open the belly. For a moment he worked on the rear and then pulled out the end of the intestines through an incision. A few quick cuts around the diaphragm, and a few more at the crotch and the old man held the full bladder. Tossing this to the ground, the plainsman turned the deer and the guts and entrails spilled out. Cutting up into the breast bone, the man reached in and pulled down the esophagus. A long corrugated white tube appeared in his hands, and now all the innards lay on the ground completely separated from the deer. The old man lifted the hindquarters so that blood drained from the open belly cavity.

"Don't waste the liver and heart," said Horse, bending down over the guts and making a few more cuts.

The oldster threw the heart and then parts of the liver into the empty cavity of the deer.

"Eddy," directed Horse. "You lay out this here tarp in the back of the wagon. Then you two boys grab the legs and throw the carcass on it. Be sure to tuck in the canvas to keep the flies out."

The two did as they were told, and then they got back aboard the wagon. Horse turned south and along the wash.

"We're gonna eat mighty fine tonight, boys!" declared Horse. "Haw, haw, haw!"

They rode some distance in silence and then Horse explained.

"We'll camp early tonight. We need to cook up that meat so it won't spoil. I don't figure anyone is following, but if they do, we'll set camp so's we're ready for 'em."

Horse did exactly as he told them. In late afternoon he headed the team to a stand of water, and let them drink. He did the same with the mustangs that had followed behind. Then he turned the wagon towards a distant hill and climbed it. On top was a copse of heavy brush and trees. Horse drove the wagon into it.

"Now you boys watch what I do and then from now on, it's your job."

The old-timer unharnessed the team. He found a sack of items he needed from the wagon, and pulled out hobbles, picket pins, and ropes. He picketed the draft horses and hobbled the mustangs. Then he had the younger men take the deer from the back of the wagon and set it some distance from camp. Horse began cutting up the meat.

"You fellers gather firewood and roll some rocks for a fire pit."

In a short time they had a fire going, the surrounding brush hiding the smoke. Horse arranged forked sticks and hung strips of venison on them above the flames. He cut up the liver and sliced the heart and placed the meat in a large iron skillet. Taking water from a barrel, he filled a coffee pot and set it to boil. In a half hour the three men were eating and drinking coffee. The plainsman cooked the rest of the meat, wrapped and placed it in a bag which he hung with a rope from the tallest tree.

There were several old logs that lay scattered. They dragged them up onto the hill to form a square barrier. Then the old man took out the rifles and laid them in a line along the logs.

"You two put out that fire. Won't never be no light at dark. The brush might hide the fire, but there's still smoke to worry on. And, at night, the glow can be seen a long ways. If we're to keep our hair, we got to mind our manners and do nothin' foolish. The rule out here is to never reveal your presence when you don't have to."

"What about when we're shooting buffalo," began Eddy, "and leaving their . . ."

"We take our chances when we're shootin' and harvestin'," replied Horse. "At night, we move off and do our best to hide our camp. And we always take to high ground. When you see buffs for the first time, you'll know why."

With nothing else left to do, the men found their bedrolls and laid them out behind the fort of logs. At dark, the old man turned in, and it wasn't long before the two young men heard him snoring.

"What do you think?" whispered Lance.

"He's a peculiar old fellow," Fast Eddy whispered back. "Full of all kinds of twists and turns. I just wish he'd take a bath."

"Do you think Miss Lilly has men after us?"

"She was plumb mad and she wanted us dead. But I been thinking on it. For her to keep her power, she has to find another man like Big Mississippi, and that will be some doing. She'll run to the law for sure, there'll be posters on us, but I don't know how much further she'll go."

"We'll have to stay away from Missouri," said Lance.

CHAPTER SIX

At sunrise they ate breakfast, hitched the horses, loaded the wagon, and descended down onto the prairie. They traveled west, looking for the migrating herd. Days passed, and then one morning they awoke surrounded by buffalo. Lance and Fast Eddy were amazed and could barely believe their eyes. Now they knew why Horse had them camp on plateaus and high hills.

For miles, as far as the eye could see, there were buffalo. They passed by, slowly grazing on the tall prairie grass. It was June and the sun had not yet baked the grass to a straw yellow. The large, horned, shaggy beasts passed along, shuffling their hooves, and kicking up a thick haze of dust. The herd contained thousands, tens of thousands, of animals, maybe more. Eddy and Lance waited and hours passed and still the buffalo grazed along on all sides. No words could describe the experience. There must have been millions in that giant herd. Towards afternoon both younger men began to actually fear the many beasts they faced.

"If that herd ever stampeded," laughed Horse, "you'd be stomped like bug juice. The horses, the wagons, everything we have would be broken to bits. Don't look away, boys, it's God's own creation. There can't be a bigger herd of animals on all the earth. A gift that won't never be wiped out."

"When do we start shooting?" asked Eddy.

"We'll let this giant herd pass," said the old man. "Many will break off to graze. We look for bunches of fifty or less. Then's the time to pick a place to make a stand, and start shootin'."

The day after the migrating herd passed southward, they found a group of thirty animals grazing in a thickly grassed meadow. Horse parked the wagon and came back after finding the buffalo.

"You two follow me," said Horse. "We'll sneak in and set up a stand. Today I'll do the shootin' and you'll see how it goes."

The three men climbed a small hill, dropped to all fours, and crawled to the top. Behind a clump of grass, Horse set up a shooting stick and with him were four rifles. Two of them were the new Sharps and two were old double triggered Hawkens .50 caliber.

"I'll shoot and you load," ordered Horse. "Always use a shooting stick. A rifle shot low to the ground carries vibration and scares away the buffs."

The leader of the herd seemed to be a large female. Horse pointed it out, along with several large males.

"It's her I shoot first," said Horse. "Now you

see me making a stand and shooting them buffs from a little under 200 yards. Get any closer and the sound of the gunshot will scare them off. For some reason, at that distance they don't seem to run from the noise, or from dead animals. It's only when they smell blood or get spooked. Sometimes it happens with no reason, but most times they just stand and takes it until I drop 'em all. You can do this day after day. The ones that escape don't seem to remember the killin' from the day before. It's mighty strange how they don't run at the first shot. Magnificent animals, but when not chased and in a herd, they're mighty dumb brutes."

"How many bullets does it take to kill a buffalo?" asked Fast Eddy.

"It takes a big caliber rifle and plenty of powder," said Horse. "But it has to be a neck shot. From experience, it's the neck shot that brings them down. You'll learn, boys, to hold your breath and squeeze. It ain't economical to shoot more than once."

The big shaggy beasts grazed the tall grass, biting and chewing as they slowly moved along. Horse found what he thought was the leader and dropped her. A few animals close by jumped or sidestepped at her sudden fall, her large weight collapsing heavily to the ground as her legs went out from under her. Horse took another rifle and fired, and this buff simply fell over sideways, with a thump. Other animals jumped, stared for a moment, and then went back to grazing. Lance and Eddy could not believe their eyes. Horse kept firing and animal after animal collapsed and fell. After more than twenty shots, a bullet entered a large male and the animal grunted. The bullet did not kill the buff, and its front legs collapsed but not its rear. The animal grunted again, turned in a circle, and its shaggy head twisted violently in the earth, kicking up dust. The herd took notice and then one animal grunted and started to run and the remaining ten followed. Within moments the remnants of the small herd were gone. The old man shot the big wounded male one more time, and he fell over dead.

"Now begins the real work, boys," said Horse.

Horse left the rifles, all four fully loaded, and went back for the wagon. He returned and put the weapons close to hand. He saddled one of the riding horses, a tough little mustang and brought it to the men. Then he pulled out a large bundle of skinning knives and laid them out.

"You fellers watch and learn," said Horse.

The old-timer went to the first animal and began cutting. His movements were quick and well-practiced. He had the hide cut from crotch to neck and he began skinning the beast, carefully slicing away fat and connective tissue. When he had cut all the way to the backbone, he stood up and went after the saddled horse. Using a rope,

85

he tied it to the four hooves of the buffalo and placed a loop over the pommel. The horse doing the work pulled on the rope and the dead animal slowly turned over, exposing its un-skinned side.

"You saw how I cut away the hide. Have at it, boys, and don't you be slicing holes in it. When you get the whole thing loose, she'll weigh over a hundred and fifty pounds. Call when you're finished and I'll show you how to peg it out, flesh side up. In a few days, the ones we lay out will be dried and we'll roll them lengthwise in lots of ten, tie the bale and load them on the wagon."

Lance couldn't get over the size of the creature. There was a distinct smell to the animal and exposing the guts and fresh red meat to the air sickened him. The fat was white and sticky and it too had its distinct odor. Flies began to gather, and the smell of gut and fecal matter increased as the minutes passed and the hot sun baked the dead carcasses. The useless waste immediately made Lance regret ever agreeing to the task at hand. Still, he cut at the hide, breathing shallowly, and finishing as quickly as he could.

They worked at it the rest of the afternoon. Horse could skin two animals to every one that Fast Eddy and Lance labored on. By evening, they had twenty-one hides staked out, flesh side up. It was a disturbing sight to see the white hides baking in the sun. Worse were the bloody naked carcasses of the dead buffalo, giant humps of flesh on their sides, indiscriminately lying in the grass. Black horns gleamed in the sun, their shaggy heads still with the fur on, revealing what were once splendid living beasts.

"Good job, boys," said Horse. "We'll camp on that rise over yonder and try to stay close until the hides are dry. The wolves, coyotes, and other critters will be busy chewing on the meat and leave the hides alone. For the most part."

"How can you be proud of something like this?" asked Lance, revealing his disgust.

"That's money, son," said Horse, "free for the taking."

"It's not right," replied Lance. "No man should kill and make such waste."

"You signed on, big man, and you'll do the work or . . ."

"I'll do it," said Lance, "but I don't have to like it."

"There are many things in life a man does . . . and liking has nothin' to do with it," said Horse.

They camped for the night on a slight knoll near the staked hides. After breakfast of buffalo steak, Horse rode out looking for another small herd. He wasn't gone long.

"I found a bunch of about twenty," he said. "I'll take a stand and shoot again today. I'll do that this morning by myself. When the shooting stops, you bring the wagon and we'll cut up the hides. When it's done, in the afternoon, I'll have you two practice shootin'. I figure by dark that you boys will have the knack."

When the gunshots ended, Lance drove the wagon and Eddy rode the other mustang toward the rifle fire. They found Horse and in the distance they saw more than twenty downed buffalo, their dark fur rustling in the wind under the hot sun. Again, they went to skinning. It was a dirty, laborious, disgusting job.

"This sure is rotten work," complained Eddy, brushing away the swarm of flies.

"I don't know what is worse," said Lance, "the stink or the sight of them lying dead without their fur on."

Fast Eddy looked over from the buff he was skinning and nodded his head. Both men were already covered in gore, their clothes stained red from the previous day and the morning's work. Horse cut the fur off the dead animals and again he managed to be twice as fast as the young men. In the afternoon, they finished staking out the hides, wet side up. Lance went to a water barrel and began trying to clean the blood and gore off his hands.

"That there water is for drinkin', not for cleanin'," said Horse.

"I have to wash this stink off," said Lance.

"Want to do that, do what the buffs do. Roll around in the grass, use the sand, but wastin' our drinkin' water ain't it."

Lance stopped using water and he tried wiping his hands and arms clean on the tall prairie grass. Eddy gathered clumps and attempted to clean his hands and arms as well. Then he used bundles of stems to wipe at his blood-soaked clothes.

"This doesn't remove the smell," said Fast Eddy.

"First water hole we reach, we'll wash up," said Lance. "But I don't think I'll ever get the stink out of my nostrils."

"Haw, haw, haw!" laughed Horse. "You tenderfoots haven't even started! Wait till the clothes you're wearing can stand up and walk by themselves, and then you'll be *real* buff hunters!"

After a brief rest, Horse began to instruct both younger men on the finer art of loading and firing a Sharps .44. He gave each man one of the rifles and had him load and began firing.

"You ain't holding your breath and squeezing the trigger. You got to hold steady and wish the bullet to your mark. Do what I tell ya! Look . . . you put the sights on your target. You take a big breath, hold it, and slowly squeeze the trigger and let the rifle go off by itself."

It took dozens of shots before Lance and his partner began to hit their mark. It was evident that Lance was going to be the better marksman.

"Eddy, you don't listen," said Horse. "Maybe you better pretend that target yonder is one of those men who's chasing you down. It's you or him. First man that hits its mark, lives. He who don't, dies. You got to feel where that bullet goes. Keep shootin' the way you do, and someday when it counts, you'll miss and end up dead."

After that advice Eddy concentrated more and for the first time began to hit a piece of buffalo hide Horse had marked and pinned onto a dead buffalo.

"All right, boys," said Horse. "I taught you all I can teach a man using a rifle. The rest is up to you. Now let's have a go at using that big ol' Dragoon. First step is learning to load."

Lance had no trouble holding the heavy Colt .44 pistol. It fit perfectly in his large hand as if specially made for him. It didn't take long and he was hitting his target at forty feet. The same pistol was too big for Fast Eddy. To fire it, he had to hold it with both hands, and the heavy recoil made the pistol twist in his grasp. Only after he lost his fear of handling the weapon, was he able to hit the target.

"You need a lighter pistol, Eddy," said Horse. "But that there Dragoon will be mighty handy in a pinch. It can knock down anything you shoot at, and believe me, for man, bear, or buffalo, that there is some shooter."

Again they camped atop a knoll near to the latest stand.

"First time I ate a buff steak, I thought it was the best meat I ever tasted," said Fast Eddy. "That distinct sweet flavor, never thought I would ever tire of it. But eating this meat three times a day is getting old."

"Git used to it," said Horse. "We got to make the supplies we brought last. We got all that free meat and we ain't going to throw it out."

Towards evening, clouds began to form on the southern horizon. Near dark there was a low rumble of thunder and a flash of light.

"Boys," said Horse, "looks like we're in for a blow."

"Good," said Lance. "Give us a chance to get clean."

"Storms out here can be dangerous," said the old-timer. "Rain can flood a plain and fill a dry wash to a raging river, wind can blow a man down, lightning can cleave a tree. I seen where it started grass fires that blow across the land as fast as a man can run, and boys, you don't never want to be caught in one of them. If lightning starts to strike, run for it. Them iron tires on the wagon, and those rifles, can draw lightning like a mother to a child."

From their camp they watched the distant storm pass to the south and once again the sun peeked through thick clouds. Then a large patch of blue appeared as the sun set.

"Looks like the storm passed us," said Horse.

Tired and having nothing else to do, they turned in for the night.

"Can't hardly stand this stink," said Lance. "Hope it rains tonight after all; maybe they'll be a pond and we can wash up in the morning."

The oldster laid out the rifles as he did every night, loaded and ready behind a rock parapet. The old man always demanded that some type of fort or barrier be built. Some encampments had no trees or rocks and then Horse would make Eddy and Lance dig a hole.

"Got to be prepared," explained Horse.

The frontiersman seemed to never have trouble sleeping. For a man who was careful on the plains, he sure snored loudly. Eventually Eddy and Lance fell asleep.

A terrific blast broke the quiet of the night, making dark into daylight, shaking the ground, and deafening the three men. Horse was immediately up and yelling.

"Lightning!" screamed the old man. "Knock those rifles down and push that wagon off the hill!"

More lightning strikes hit, one after another, and it seemed as if the night was gone. Arcs of light, too intense for the eyes to endure, lit up the sky. The dark image of the old man was brightly exposed as he stood knocking over the line of rifles. A lightning bolt struck the top of Horse's head. The bright electric flash tore through his body, smoke billowed, raised his hair, tore his clothing, and the bolt exited and traveled along the ground. In the flash of light, both Eddy and Lance, still on their bedrolls, clearly saw the gruesome sight. Then other lightning bolts struck, hit the wagon repeatedly, and fire erupted around an iron wheel. More smoke billowed and flames spread across the wagon.

Eddy hurried to Horse and then lightning struck again and Eddy fell. Lance jumped from his blankets and raced to Eddy, threw him over his shoulders and ran down the hill. At the bottom, he placed Eddy on the ground. They both lay prone as the lightning and blowing storm raged around them. At the top of the hill, grass was now burning as well as the wagon, and a wind blew at a terrific force, howling fiercely. Flames pushed down the hill and towards where the two men lay. Once again, Lance picked up his partner and in bare feet hurried away from the rushing fire.

A wall of flames headed toward Lance and he feared that they would overtake them. This was exactly as the old man had described. Lightning flashed once more at the top of the hill, a terrific fork of white-hot heat, followed by deafening thunder. Then it was as if the sky cracked in two, and a cascade of water fell, drenching the flames. The water poured as if thrown from buckets and in a moment the dry ground turned to grease. Sticky mud slid under Lance's bare feet and he fell, Eddy coming down hard on top of him.

The fall brought the other man to consciousness.

"What? What's happened?" asked Eddy.

"Lightning struck and knocked you out," shouted Lance above the sound of the wind and pouring rain. "It started a fire and I picked you up and ran."

They both stared up at the knoll and, despite the heavy rain, areas of grass, bushes, and the wagon were still engulfed in flames. As the rain poured on, they watched the fires ebb and then go out.

"Did you see the old man?" asked Eddy. "He . . . he was struck in the head. I saw the bolt go through him and then hit and travel along the ground. He fell and when I ran towards him there was smoke . . ."

"I saw it too," said Lance. "Let's wait the storm out and . . ."

A terrific wind blew and water struck their faces and stung. Both men lay flat along the ground and put arms over their heads to protect themselves. Then as quickly as it came, the storm moved off. Lightning strikes moved with it, and then further and further away, until it was only a distant flash and low rumble. The wind stopped and with it the rain. Both men sat up and stared into inky blackness. A few flashes more, a distant clap of thunder, and the storm was gone.

"Come on," said Lance, "maybe we can save the old man."

In the distance the sun slowly formed a thin

94

orange disk on the horizon and the darkness fled. Clouds swirled above and began to quickly dissipate. Blue sky appeared and the sun began to rise. Orange rays were replaced with bright yellow. Daylight flooded across the land.

Fast Eddy and Lance, both barefooted, slogged across slippery adobe mud. It stuck to their feet in great clumps and they had to stop from time to time to shove the sticky clay off. Eventually they came to the hill. Behind them they left deep holes where they walked. With difficulty they climbed the hill and saw where the old man lay. Lance reached him first and bent down. Gently he turned Horse over, and what they saw sickened both of them.

The lightning had burned the frontiersman horribly. There was a rifle below part of his body and the metal of the barrel was bent and the wood exploded from the stock. Parts of the old man's shirt was charred, his skin was blotchy and red, and the top of his head and face badly seared.

"Killed him, right off," said Eddy.

"Yeah," said Lance.

The two draft horses that were picketed at the very center of the hill both lay on their sides. Lance walked over and saw that they too were dead. The mustangs that were hobbled were nowhere to be seen.

"The riding horses are gone," said Lance.

"Look at the wagon," said Eddy. "It and the

supplies are burned to a crisp. Horse sure was telling the truth when . . ."

"We got to find what we can save out of this mess, and then hope the horses are all right," said Lance.

"They couldn't have gotten too far," said Fast Eddy. "I hobbled them myself."

The men slogged around camp trying to salvage what they could. They found socks and their boots and put them on. Searching, they gathered up two Sharps rifles and the three Dragoon pistols, still intact. The other rifles were burned or damaged in some way. A few beans remained on the ground and these Fast Eddy picked up and placed in a sack. Gradually the hot sun began to bake the soft ground and within hours it was easier to walk around.

"I'll go look for the horses," said Lance. "You try to put what can be saved together."

"There ain't much," said Eddy. "What didn't burn or was struck by lightning, was blown away with the wind. Even our bedrolls and blankets are gone."

"I found the saddles and tack," said Lance. "Now all I got to do is find the horses."

By evening Lance returned with the mounts.

"Where'd you find them?" asked Fast Eddy.

"I went in the wrong direction," replied Lance. "By the time I made a full circle I found them down in a low place chomping grass like there was nothing wrong. They acted glad to see me. There's a big pond over there. I took the time to bathe and wash my clothes. You might want to do the same."

"While you were gone and before the ground got hard," said Eddy, "I dug a hole and put Horse in it. I figured maybe you and me could put up a marker and say a few words over him."

Lance stuck a broken rifle in the ground at the head of the grave and fixed a stick to it to make a cross. Eddy watched and then both men stood over the mound.

"You know more about the Good Book than I do," said Fast Eddy.

"Horse," began Lance. "We never got that chance for you to teach me to read. Overall I think you were what Mammy would call a good man. Maybe this was the Lord's way of telling us it was wrong to shoot all those fine buffalo. I remember Mammy reading from Ecclesiastes . . . *All go unto one place; all are of the dust, and all turn to dust again.* Amen."

"Amen," repeated Fast Eddy.

They spent the night at the top of the knoll and in the morning packed up and went to the pond. In rummaging through the mess on the hill, Eddy found one cake of lye soap. He used it to wash the blood and gore from himself and his clothes. The remainder Lance used on himself.

"I tell you," said Eddy. "I feel like a new man."

"Surprising what a little soap and water can do," agreed Lance.

"It's a shame that we can't roll up those hides and sell them . . . 'specially after all that work of skinning them."

"I feel better that we can't," said Lance.

"Which way do we go now?"

Both men mounted their horses.

"Do we have a choice?" asked the big man. "We can't go back to St. Louis."

"But there's Indians out there. What chance do we have without someone like Horse?"

"All I know is that I'm not going back. You can go where you want, but I'm heading west to California."

"I thought we were friends. You wouldn't leave me? Not after saving my life?"

"You would have done the same thing," said Lance.

"I might have tried, but I'm afraid there's no way I could have picked you up, let alone run down that hill."

"I never had a friend," said Lance. "Just what do you mean by it?"

"Why Lance," said Fast Eddy. "A friend is . . . why . . . I never had to describe it before. Let me think . . ."

"Like I said," replied Lance. "I never had a friend before. And you don't know what it means either."

"I do so!" said Eddy with some heat. "A friend is someone who stands by you. Who watches your back when you're in trouble. Who . . . who carries you off a hill during a lightning strike and saves your life. A true friend is a pal who never lets his buddy down . . . no matter what."

"Is that how you feel?" asked Lance. "Or are you just saying words?"

"Lance! Look at all we've been through together! You saved my life! Of course they're not just words. I mean everything I said."

Lance stopped his horse, turned, and brought it close to Eddy's. The tall giant stared down at his companion. Some seconds ticked by, then showing great emotion, Lance stuck out a huge right hand. Eddy looked back, mouth open in surprise. Then he smiled and put out a smaller hand in return. Lance shook it and squeezed hard. Wincing from the pain of it, Fast Eddy did his best to increase his grip. Lance let go and Eddy sighed in relief.

"What do you think it all means, Eddy?" asked Lance, sitting on the mustang looking up at the great dome of the open sky.

His horse nervously shook its head against flies, and long moments passed before Eddy responded. "What you referring to, Lance? You mean all this? Smarter fellers than us have been asking that question . . ."

Lance nodded his head.

"I don't know, sometimes when I was working the fields or the worst times when they tied me to a whipping post . . . or the good times when Mammy read from the Good Book . . . I wondered," said Lance. "Mammy, she said it wasn't for man to understand everything but just to have faith. Do you have faith, Eddy?"

"I reckon in my own way I do," said Fast Eddy. "We're born, we get dealt the cards we're gonna hold . . . we struggle . . . and die. I've been thinkin' on it. Horse, as mean or as hard as he sometimes was, didn't have it coming the way he got it."

"I agree," said Lance. "He didn't."

Fast Eddy's horse jumped as though bitten and Lance's black mustang followed and both animals began a walk. Their noses were pointed northwest, and neither rider corrected their direction.

CHAPTER SEVEN

On their first day of travel their own blankets and canvas were found snagged on bushes. With warm bedrolls they did not suffer privation. Reluctant to shoot any more of the great buffalo, Eddy and Lance instead lived off mule deer and the vast herds of antelope they encountered. There were rabbits in plenty, and they never went hungry. Water was harder to find than food, and the men kept their canteens full.

They journeyed cautiously across the vast open spaces of the Great Plains. Following what they learned from Horse, every evening they camped on high ground and never lit a fire after dark. Several times they saw Indians and avoided them. Both men learned to study the land and to ride and keep hidden as best they could.

From a distance the country looked flat and endless—a vast sea of waving grassland that went clear to the horizon in every direction. It was a deception that the land was flat. Instead it rolled in great waves, contained hidden valleys, hollows, deep ravines, washes, escarpments, and odd formations. They learned to train their eyesight, and by keen observation could see moving objects miles away. This was truly a wild and unexplored plain that required caution in traversing.

They had been traveling in a steady northwest direction and one day they came upon a wide area where the grass was eaten down. Exploring further, they discovered a trail, heavily used, with iron wagon wheels making marks in the soil.

"What do you think it is?" asked Fast Eddy.

"Quite a number of wagons going west," said Lance. "The stock have eaten the grass on both sides of the trail."

"Why are so many folks traveling?"

"I don't know," replied Lance. "I have an idea if we follow, we'll find out."

Gunshots echoed across the land. Climbing a hill, Fast Eddy and Lance looked down on a group of wagons. Men were indiscriminately shooting buffalo and letting the animals lie where they fell.

"The fools," said Lance, in as angry a voice as Fast Eddy had ever heard him speak.

Lance prodded his heels into the black mustang's sides and it jumped to a lope and then a full gallop.

"Stop!" shouted Lance, and his voice was loud and carried to the caravan.

Men stopped shooting. Lance charged down upon them. Fast Eddy was too surprised to follow. He watched and wondered if his friend would be shot. Eddy held his breath. Men aimed their rifles at Lance and then held their fire as the young giant continued to yell his displeasure.

"Quit that!" shouted Lance.

"What's the matter with you, mister?" asked a tall black-bearded man.

The wagon train halted and the bearded fellow jumped down. He held a rifle in his hands.

"You're killing just to kill!" shouted Lance, dismounting from his horse and confronting the big stranger.

"What makes it your business?"

"You're wasting good meat."

"Mister," said the angry fellow. "No one comes charging in here and tells me what to do."

"I just did," said Lance, advancing closer.

"Then you can die, you fool," he said, pointing his rifle.

Lance's fist struck out and into the man's face. The fellow acted as if a sledgehammer had struck and he fell to the ground and did not move. Men came from various wagons and instead of anger, Lance encountered smiles and several of the group thumped him on his back.

"Good to see you, feller," said one.

"You gave him what for," smiled another. "About time he got what he had coming."

A horse trotted up behind Lance and he turned to see who it was. Fast Eddy jumped down and he also was greeted by the gathering group.

"What's going on here?" asked Eddy.

"That there feller is Blacky Schmidt," explained a middle-aged man with red hair. "Back a ways he showed up and asked to be part of our group. We didn't know him and said no. He kept after us 'til we finally voted and let him join. At first things were fine, but pretty soon he started threatening us, and backing it up with his fists and guns. 'Til that big friend of yours came along, we've been plumb feared what to do."

"He tried to shoot me," said Lance.

"Might be better if you shot him dead," continued the red-haired man. "Don't have no idea what he'll do when he wakes. But it won't be good."

"Why are so many of you travelling west?" asked Eddy.

"Haven't you heard? There's gold in Californy."

"No, we haven't," replied Eddy.

"Where you been?" asked Red. "Why, the whole country is talking about it."

"There can't be that much gold," said Eddy. "Not for all."

"Why, there is! We heard tell you can walk along and pick nuggets off the ground. Not counting Blacky, there's seventeen of us, and we're going to share every piece of gold we dig up! Why don't you two fellers come with us and join in. We're going to be rich!"

Blacky Schmidt began to make sounds and

seemed to be coming to. He moved his head slowly and groaned and then all of a sudden he jumped to his feet, a large knife in his right hand.

"Let me at him!" growled Blacky. "I'll cut him to pieces."

An old, grey-haired man dressed in buckskins, poked Blacky hard in the back with the end of his rifle barrel and then jumped back. The bully turned menacingly and sliced air with his knife, missing the oldster by a foot.

"Hey! That hurt!" shouted Blacky. "I'll git you too, old man!"

"The name's Horntoad Harry and you know it!" exclaimed the frontiersman. "And you ain't gittin no one, nowhere, no how! Thanks to that giant feller over there, your pushing us around ends right here and right now. He taught us that your meat house can be knocked down like any other man."

"Where is he?" shouted Blacky. "Just let me fight him again and I'll show who's boss!"

"I'm right here," said Lance, walking forward and facing the big man."

"I'm going to slice you wide open . . ."

.From behind, the old-timer struck Blacky on the head with his rifle barrel, and the blow made a loud hollow sound. The troublemaker fell once more, out cold.

"You might of beat him," said Horntoad Harry,

"but he wasn't playing fair, and 'sides, I'd hate to see a big feller like you all cut up for no reason a'tall."

"Horntoad is a real plainsman, he joined our group a while back," said the red-headed man. "Let me introduce all around. My name's Red, that feller over there is Jake, that's Zeke, Hezekiah, and, well, let the others tell you. And you two?"

"I'm Lance, and my friend is Fast Eddy."

The newcomers shook hands all around and names were again exchanged.

"How about we tie Blacky up," said Red. "We can unload his guns, set him on his horse, and make him ride in another direction."

"What's to keep him from drygulching one of us, first chance he gits?" asked Horntoad. "I say we break a leg or put a hole in him, to give him somethin' else to think on."

"No matter how bad he is or what thoughts he has about our gold, we can't do something like that," replied Red.

Blacky groaned once more and then slowly sat up, rubbing his head. Several of the men had already emptied Blacky's saddle pistols and rifle. Another took his horse from behind a wagon and saddled it.

"I should have thumped him harder," complained Horntoad Harry.

"Blacky," said Red. "Here's your horse, your

pistols, and your rifle. Mount up and ride out!"

Sixteen voices murmured unanimous consent.

"I ain't goin' nowhere," said Blacky. Then he drew a large single-shot pistol from his saddle holster.

Everyone heard the hammer and saw his finger on the trigger.

"Won't do you any good," said Red. "Your guns are empty."

Blacky pointed the barrel at Red and pulled the trigger. It merely clicked.

"Told you," said Red. "Now get going!"

Those men with rifles pointed them at the big man. Blacky looked around in a full circle and grinned.

"I wondered when any of you would have the sand to stand up to me. You never would have if it wasn't for that big feller."

"No talk," ordered Horntoad. "Ride!"

"I'll be seeing you men. You just watch for me and when you least expect it, I'll be there to throw this in your face. Then I'll break it!"

"Blacky, you're a mean-mouthed, low-down, ornery skunk," said Horntoad. "In my younger days I'd have taken you on in a knife fight and I would have sliced your ears off and gutted you like a prime beaver."

Blacky took the reins of his horse and mounted. Someone handed him his empty rifle and the big, bearded man looked down.

"Brave talk, old man. I'll be looking for you special."

"You polecat!" shouted Horntoad. "Move on or I'll drill you 'tween the eyes!"

Blacky made a loud snickering sound with his mouth and then dug heels into his horse. Pulling reins, the troublemaker turned his mount west and rode away. The group watched until horse and man disappeared into a low spot on the horizon.

"I'm afeared," said the old-timer, "that we're gonna regret not killin' that *hombre*."

"You men that shot a buffalo," said Lance. "Suppose we take their skins, and some of the meat?"

"Good idea!" said the plainsman. "We'll be needin' meat and buffalo robes up in the mountains. This place is as good as any to tan the hides. 'Bout time I earn my keep and learn you how."

The old frontiersman, along with Lance and Eddy, showed skill in skinning the many dead buffalo. The others looked on or assisted when asked. Meat was cut and collected, some of it jerked, smoked, or cooked. It took the rest of the day to remove the twenty-some-odd hides and stake them out on the plains. Horntoad began scraping tissue and fat, and the men followed suit. When the hides were cleaned, he broke open the skulls and used brains to begin tanning.

"Learned this from the Cheyenne."

"We'll lose time getting to the gold fields," complained Red.

Through the day several small groups of men passed along the trail, many hooting back at the group of would-be miners.

"For winter we'll need buffalo coats and robes," said the plainsman. "When other men are freezing, we'll be as warm as a papoose wrapped in her mother's cradleboard."

They stayed three days and in that time the hides were partially dried and cured. Each man took one to work the leather. During the delay, the men repaired their wagons and equipment. Cooked buff was eaten. Smoked and jerked meat put away. While they worked, they saw many more wagons pass on the trail to California. Red's party bantered with the passing miners and the sense of urgency to beat others to the gold fields was still upon each man.

"Don't worry," said the plainsman. "It's a sensible thing we did here. Our horses and mules needed rest, and wagons had to be greased and repaired. We can always use meat. Opportune it was to have Lance and his friend come along."

"It goes the same for you, Horntoad," said Red. "Without your skills, it would have been a rougher trip."

"What do you mean?" asked Lance.

"When you weren't with us, back on the trail, we faced some tough going."

"So did we," replied Lance. "In a bad storm we lost a man. And you?"

"Let's just say, without Horntoad, we wouldn't have made it this far."

"This ain't the last of our troubles," interjected the plainsman. "We got to go easy on the stock and there's a real bad place ahead."

Several of Red's party gathered to listen.

"Where's that?" asked one of the men.

"Didn't want to talk of it until we got near," said the old-timer. "It'll be the hardest to cross. We got to make sure the stock is rested, watered, and in good shape."

"We don't need any more surprises," said Red. "You better explain."

"It's a desert," answered Horntoad Harry, "a real bad stretch of forty miles or more. When we come to the Humboldt River we'll have to fill every water barrel and canteen. There won't be water for quite a stretch after that. I was with Frémont when he went across that river, and it ain't no beauty. It's a muddy, slow-moving, alkaline-tasting crick. But believe me, you fellers will be glad it's there."

"And beyond the desert lies California and the gold fields!" exclaimed one of the men.

"I'm gonna be the first to pick up nuggets!" said another.

"I'm talking reality here," explained the frontiersman. "When we hit the Humboldt River and later the mountains, we got to be real careful about treatin' the stock right, or we still won't make it. We've travelled nearly fifteen hundred miles and we got more than that to go. The stock and you fellers got to stay healthy and we got to take vinegar once in a while to keep off the scurvy. Good thing I'm here to keep you greenhorns out of trouble."

"You talk like a mother hen," said Zeke. "All I want is to get to Californy and fill my pockets with gold!"

"You think it will be easy?" asked Horntoad. "Let me tell you what prospectin' is really like! You fellers can dream all you want, but you'll learn real quick how much pokin' with pick and shovel it'll take to find gold. It ain't nothin' but hard labor, pickin', diggin', shovelin', standing in ice cold streams with blistered hands, and grubbin' in gravel and mud day after day. Gold minin' ain't no fun time. I done it, and I know that it's doggone nasty work."

CHAPTER EIGHT

True to the old frontiersman's word, their stop did make a difference for the adventurous party. The rested and well-grazed stock passed other wagons with their worn-out mules, oxen, and horses. Horntoad explained to the would-be miners that they still had Sioux territory to pass through. He cautioned again about fires at night, or using a rifle and killing buffs on Indian land.

"No sense in riling the Injuns. Since leaving Fort Kearny we've been lucky. We've got a ways to go to Fort Laramie, and from there through South Pass to that there fort that Bridger built."

The men, having learned to listen to the frontiersman, made do with the food and supplies they carried. They traveled twenty miles a day and, seeing game along the trail, refrained from using their rifles. In late afternoon, dead tired, they circled their wagons and extinguished all fires before dark.

It was near Fort Laramie, in the middle of the day, they came to a long hill and at the top of it saw a party of twenty-some Indians.

"Circle the wagons!" ordered Horntoad.

The men acted on his orders. And when the task was completed, they watched the Indians approach on painted ponies.

"Keep the brakes on them wagons," whispered the plainsman. "If you don't want the stock turned into pin cushions and your hair on a pole, you men do as I say. If I tell one of you to jump, you jump. If I say fetch, you fetch. This is their land, and if you see twenty, you can bet there's a heap more of them close by. Better you let me palaver our way out of this than to fight."

The Indians rode right up to the wagons. Horntoad, Lance, and Eddy stood to greet them.

"Do you speak their language?" asked Lance.

"I know some Teton," replied Horntoad. "This here group is Oglala Sioux. Red! You fetch a blanket and set it down between us. We're gonna do some trade."

Red climbed off his seat and went through the back of his wagon and jumped down. He ran before the frontiersman and whipped the blanket out and it settled flat, without wrinkles, to the ground.

"Good!" said the old man. "Now you fellers stay up on your wagon seats real careful like, and each of you reach for a rifle. I want you to hold steady, casual like, and keep them shooters pointed at the sky. If anything goes wrong, I'll shout, and you boys shoot straight."

When the lead Indian's paint stopped ten feet from the blanket, Horntoad Harry raised a right hand and began to speak in a foreign tongue. The leader dismounted and answered in a strange high timbered voice. By now, the warriors spread out in a long mounted line, horses pawing nervously at the hard ground. Each brave held a rifle or bow in hand, with a full quiver of arrows. More words were exchanged, and then two Indians jumped down from their mounts and stood behind their leader.

"Lance, you and Eddy stand behind me. Hold your rifles up and don't move. Pretend you're guardin' me . . . 'cause you are."

The plainsman flourished hand and arm courteously before the Indian leader and pointed to the blanket. Together both men sat and crossed their legs. The two sitting upon the blanket began to speak and sign.

"The rascal's asking us why so many are passing through their land," Horntoad explained to the men. "I told him we're headed for Californy. He wants to know why. I told him for the land. He doesn't like that. He says we're trespassin', scarin' game, makin' a nuisance."

Again the two leaders upon the blanket spoke for long moments, continuing to sign.

"Red!" shouted Horntoad. "Bring me an axe for payment. Be quick about it, and place it in the middle of the blanket."

One more time, Red put down his rifle, climbed over the seat and into the back of his wagon. Within seconds he came running with a large axe and set it in the middle of the blanket. Each group heard the Indian leader grunt and saw him shake his head.

"Now listen here," said Horntoad. "Red, you go among the men and gather two tobacco pouches, two knives, and two iron skillets. Don't dally."

Red ran back to his wagon yet again, climbed up and loudly searched among his possessions. He jumped down with a skillet and two knives. Passing other wagons, he was given another skillet and two tobacco pouches. Red moved hurriedly and then ran back and deftly placed the items in the middle of the blanket. Again both parties heard the Indian grunt in the negative.

"Boys!" said the frontiersman. "This here Indian is named Red Cloud. I heard of him and he's rising quick in the Sioux nation as a leader. He says he wants guns and a couple mules. We ain't gonna give 'em. You men stand quick, and don't fool yourselves; some of these warriors speak American as good as you 'n me."

Again Horntoad and Red Cloud exchanged words and sign, and this time they both spoke louder and in argument.

"Red!" shouted the old man. "Run and fetch that buffalo coat I finished and left in the back of your wagon."

Red ran and did as ordered, but this time handed the coat to Horntoad. The plainsman stood and held the softly tanned and heavy coat before the Indian. He put it on to show how it fit, and to display its fine detail. Then he removed it and placed it on top of the blanket. Again, Red Cloud grunted. Horntoad made a level sweep of his hand and all saw that the gift giving was finished.

The old frontiersman nodded his head, folded his arms, and remained standing. Finally, Red Cloud nodded his head in assent and then rose and extended his right arm. The two leaders grasped hand over wrist and shook.

Suddenly, an angry young warrior jumped from his horse and yelled in a burst of loud and rapid Sioux. He came forward and pointed at the party of miners and made fierce gestures, continuing to shout. Red Cloud gave orders and the two Indians behind him grabbed the young warrior and dragged him away.

"That," explained Horntoad Harry, "was a little devil called Likes-To-Fight. Red Cloud says the young buck bit a live rattlesnake last week and he's been a bit tempered since. Indian humor, boys! Haw! Haw! Haw! They're going to let us go! Don't make no sudden moves!"

Another Indian came and took up the heavy buffalo coat and ran back to his horse. Still another folded up the blanket with the gifts inside and carried them to his pony. Mounted, Red Cloud gave a final salute. The painted horses turned in unison, leaped into a gallop, and within moments the Indians disappeared in a cloud of dust over the hill.

"You men done fine," complimented the plainsman.

"But I gave up my favorite blanket," complained Red.

The men, immensely relieved, put down their rifles and laughed.

More wary now, with the experience of encountering the Sioux, the miners traveled as quietly as they could through the vast plains. Under the frontiersman's urging they passed by Fort Laramie and continued on. Days turned into weeks. They came to Independence Rock and finally South Pass. When they reached Fort Bridger they stayed and rested several days. At the fort, they warily eyed the many parties of would-be miners who passed them by. Red and his men remained restless. At the same time they realized the prospectors they saw were foolishly pushing themselves and their stock beyond all reason.

"Mark my words," said Horntoad. "Many of them fellers ain't gonna make it."

Lance was walking by the miners with Eddy, and the frontiersman followed.

"I been looking for a chance to talk," said the old man. "I wanted to say that I like the way you two handle yourselves. Lance, no man would argue that it took a feller of your size to take down that Blacky. Ever since, I been thinkin'. You two are just the hombres I been lookin' to join up with. Together, the three of us could make some real money in those gold fields."

"What do you have in mind?" asked Lance.

"Like I said," replied Horntoad, "gold minin' ain't no fun. When we get to Californy, suppose we find an easier way of earnin' coin? I'm not getting any younger, and some day I'd like to settle down on some ranch."

"It depends on what you have in mind," said Eddy. "But I'm willing to listen if Lance is."

"Good, then we'll talk on it some more later," replied the old-timer.

The next morning, refreshed, the party of twenty men, led by Horntoad Harry, headed to Fort Hall and the turnoff to the California Trail. Traversing twenty miles each weary day, they finally came to the Humboldt River. It was a depressing, low-lying, slow-moving, muddy stream. Grass and sage enclosed the water, and there wasn't a tree to be seen. Next to the river was an encampment of four wagons and picketed mules. There was one fire smoldering but no people moving about. Then they heard a woman scream.

"Somethin's wrong," mumbled Horntoad. "Red, you keep the men and the stock away from the river until I find out what it is."

The grizzled frontiersman lifted his rifle to

leave and then turned to Lance and Fast Eddy.

"I got a bad feelin'. I sure hope you two know how to use them rifles, 'cause you're going with me."

They walked a hundred yards to the wagons. Horntoad pointed for Lance to go around to the right and Eddy to the left.

"If I shoot, you shoot," whispered the buck-skinned plainsman.

Horntoad held his rifle at the ready and walked silently toward the wagons; the younger men followed his lead. The vehicles blocked the fire and as he came closer he distinctly heard a slapping sound and then a female cry out again. Sneaking between two wagons he saw three men standing by the river, close to a woman and a child. One man was shaking the woman and then he slapped her repeatedly.

"Tell me where's the money. Speak up or . . ."

"Grab the kid," said another of the men. "She'll talk then."

"Please," begged the mother. "My father, the other men, they're dying. You can't do . . ."

"You talk or the kid gets it," threatened the thief.

One of the outlaws attempted to grab the young boy. The child dodged and ran straight towards Horntoad Harry, who now was standing with rifle raised and aimed at the leader. The three thieves saw him. The leader of the group reached for a pistol at his belt, and Horntoad fired. Blood splattered from the man's chest and he fell. The other two robbers held rifles and they raised them to shoot. From either side of the wagon, guns fired, and the thieves dropped.

"Johnny!" screamed the young woman.

The boy, four or five years old, turned and ran into his mother's arms. Picking up the child she held him close.

"Didn't mean to scare you, ma'am," said Horntoad Harry. "I had a feeling somethin' was wrong. Did them skunks hurt you?"

"No, but they were going to . . ."

"Lance," said the plainsman. "You and Eddy take one of those picketed mules, and drag those three dead critters and chuck 'em in a hole. Make sure it's far from the water."

"They were trying to rob us," cried the woman. "They wouldn't let me explain we didn't have much . . . that awful man was . . ."

"I saw and heard, ma'am," replied Horntoad. "You're safe. Now what's happened to your men?"

"They got sick," answered the woman. "I told Father the water looked bad. I told them to boil it before drinking . . . I did that for Johnny and me and . . ."

"They got sick and you didn't?"

"That's right."

"Excuse my manners, ma'am. Folks call me Horntoad Harry, and you?"

"I'm Katherine, and this is Johnny, my son. Everyone calls me Katy."

"Tell me how long you've been here?"

"Weeks," she responded.

"When did they get sick and how many?"

"I'm a widow. There's Father, my two uncles, and two other friends. We were going to stay about a week to rest the mules and repair the wagons. After five days one of the men became ill and then within a few more days all of them. I've been caring for them and trying to keep Johnny from . . ."

"Can I have a look?" asked the old man.

Katy pointed toward a wagon.

"My father's in that one."

Horntoad pulled back canvas and began to climb up. Immediately the odor of vomit and soiled bedding struck his nose and it was overwhelming. Turning back and taking a breath of air, the old-timer held it and climbed back up. Bending down he saw the bluish color and sunken flesh of an older man. The frontiersman quickly exited the wagon.

"It's cholera," he told the young woman.

"Oh!" she said. "Was it the water?"

"Yes, something dead in the stagnant water. Better you not drink any more of it. Best you move further upstream."

"But I can't," said Katy. "I'm exhausted. I tried to help them but no matter what I do I can't keep up and they're getting worse."

"Where do you keep your boy?"

"We've been sleeping outside and . . ."

The woman sat down on a water keg next to the wagon. Eddy and Lance came back with a mule and loaded the last of the three dead men on it.

"Wait here," the plainsman said. "I have to get back to my wagon train. I'll give them instructions and return. It won't be long."

Horntoad hurried. Red and the men were waiting. He told them what happened and to lead the wagons at least a mile upstream and camp.

"Try to find a spring if you can," said the old man. "But be sure to boil all the water. Start filling every water keg and canteen and we'll rest and decide when to start across the desert."

"What about the cholera, that woman, and those men?" asked Red. "Will you . . . we . . . catch it?"

"Not if we're careful," replied Horntoad. "I'm gonna help those folks, best I can. Now that I think on it, leave me soap, a roll of canvas, and some food."

When Horntoad Harry returned, Lance and Fast Eddy were talking to Katy. Lance was seated on a box, and the five-year-old boy was sitting comfortably on his knee. The giant's stature was muted by the boy's presence. The big man's face was gentle and it was evident that a great need was being fulfilled. The old frontiersman knew immediately that he had lost this young man to the boy and his mother.

"Katy was telling me you said it was cholera," said Lance. "We waited for you to come and tell us what to do."

"I've been thinkin' on it," replied Horntoad. "I know somethin' about this."

"Well?" asked Lance.

"I see Miss Katy done her best, but judging from her father's condition, he's pretty well gone . . ."

There was a suppressed cry from the young woman.

"Those men have drunk bad water. Probably some dead man or animal in that slow-moving stream. There's a whole bunch of things that need to be done."

Fast Eddy, Katy, and Lance leaned closer to catch the frontiersman's words.

"First thing is to get that boy away from this camp. I don't know how many days I can keep Red and his men upstream, but I'll stay and help as long as I can. One of you has to remain with the boy and keep him from catching this. It will kill him sure if . . ."

"I can't leave my father," said Katy.

"Then . . . one of you . . ."

"Let Eddy stay with Johnny," said Lance. "I'll help you and Katy."

The three men looked to the mother and she nodded her head.

"All right, then," said Horntoad. "From what I know, the sick have to be gotten out of the wagons and put on somethin' like canvas. They got to be stripped and kept clean by using soap and buckets of water. I don't know what you did, ma'am, but you need plenty of lye soap and to keep your hands clean. You can't touch none of that filth coming from them or you'll catch it. The wagons and the beddings got the disease and needs to be burned."

Katy gasped at this.

"Can't be helped, ma'am," explained the old man. "Eddy can go upstream and fetch water back, but it's got to be boiled before drinkin'. If we're gonna save any of these men we got to try to get water with some salt into them. Get them to eat if we can. From what a doc told me once, it's the loss of water and food that's killin' em, and no matter how much they throw up, or what comes out of 'em, we got to try to git it back in. If we don't, they'll die."

"What about the things we brought with us? Can anything be saved?" asked Katy.

"Guns, and what can be washed," said Horntoad. "Anything that's been soiled, including the wagons, has to be burned. You got plenty of mules to carry supplies. Best the stock be moved upstream with Eddy and the boy."

As they were talking, a group of wagons came along the trail. When they drove closer, Horntoad yelled.

"Cholera! Go 'round!"

Hearing the frontiersman's call, the party of five wagons and men sitting up on them halted.

"We need water!" called the lead driver.

"Best go upstream!" shouted Horntoad. "Boil your water!"

"All right, mister!" shouted the man, and the wagons turned off the trail and headed north.

"We need to put up a yellow flag and a sign saying cholera," suggested Horntoad Harry. "Might want to add 'Bad Water.'"

"I've got a yellow kerchief," said Katy. "And I can make the sign."

"We still got more to do," said the plainsman, his red wrinkled face frowning and showing tough as tanned leather.

CHAPTER NINE

Fast Eddy took the sign and yellow kerchief and went up the trail, placed a post in the ground, and secured flag and notice. Returning, he gathered the boy and the mules, loaded empty water kegs, and moved upstream. He established another camp, built a fire, and began boiling water. When the kegs were filled, he returned.

In Eddy's absence, Horntoad and Lance got the canvas. From one large piece they cut up sections, placed them on the ground, and pegged them down. Then they carried out the sick men. Two of them, the young men who had joined along the trail, were both lying dead in their wagon. Taking a shovel, Lance dug a grave as far from the stream as he could get, and buried the bodies and said a few words. Now it was Katy's father and her two uncles who remained. They were placed on the canvas, stripped of their clothes by Lance, and then washed down with buckets of water and lye soap.

Katy kept water boiling in a kettle. The plainsman added salt to the bowls of water, and once they had cooled, went to each sick man, and tried to get him to drink. What liquid they drank, they threw up. Lance washed the men off and then discreetly covered them with a strip of extra canvas.

As Horntoad Harry administered to the men, Katy and Lance went through the wagons, avoiding the soiled conditions as best they could. They removed guns, pots and pans, and many ordinary supplies such as kerosene, shovels, picks, and sundries. All food supplies left in the wagons would be burned. A few gold and silver coins were taken from the men's clothing and dumped in kerosene. A large pile of goods was collected and set aside. Then one by one, Lance burned the wagons. The last and best he could not bring himself to destroy. Using kerosene, he poured it on the soiled boards, and scrubbed them. Horntoad Harry looked on and commented.

"You take a chance, lad."

Katy and Lance followed the old man's instructions and washed their hands with lye soap. Eddy, feeling guilty, stood guard over the boy. From some distance, Johnny and his new caretaker watched the three work over the sick men.

As Lance, Katy, and Horntoad labored, they saw and heard groups of travelers rattle by— scattered bunches of men headed for the California gold fields. Seeing the warning, these men skirted the camp and moved on to find water up- or downstream.

"You think those folks will boil their water?" asked Lance.

"If they don't, they're fools," replied Horntoad.

As the sun set, Eddy took the boy upstream to the new camp. The old plainsman had been trying all day to get Katy's father and his two brothers to drink and eat. He had little success and what they did drink, they spewed up. Lance lit a fire. Around it, Katy and the old man sat. The three sick men remained on the canvas, their bodies repeatedly cleaned and washed. It was a symptom of the disease that kept them vomiting and suffering from diarrhea.

"I'll tell it like it is, Miss Katy," said Horntoad. "None of the three can keep in food or water. They're failing. Your father's the worst and it's only a matter of time. I suggest you try to talk to him and your uncles."

Just after the old frontiersman finished talking, they heard a horse come near and stop.

"Who is it?" called Horntoad.

Lance, taking no chances, held a rifle at the ready.

"It's Red!" came a voice out of the dark. "I can't hold back the men. They filled all the water kegs, ate their fill, and are anxious to get going. They voted, and said if you wouldn't lead us by early morning . . . well . . . we're pulling out."

"These folks are hurtin'," replied Horntoad Harry. "Can't you men have the decency to wait?

You leavin' tomorrow won't change nothin'.'"

"I tried to tell them that," said Red. "But they keep seeing all those prospectors pushing up the trail and they're worried they'll miss out."

"You tell them without me guiding 'em, it'll go harder?"

"I did."

"This here ain't right," said Horntoad. "Two men died and we got three more real sick. Lance and Fast Eddy are helping this woman and her child. I figure they won't leave 'em."

"That's right," said Lance, out of the darkness.

"Then they'll miss out on the gold," replied Red.

"You're a hard-hearted bunch," said the frontiersman.

"What's it going to be?" called Red.

"You tell 'em, if I'm there in the morning, they'll know it, and if I ain't they'll know that too."

"Lance!" called Red.

"Yeah?"

"I'm mighty sorry about this. As leader, I sure wish you and your friend were with us." Lance didn't reply, and eventually Red called out. "We need you, Horntoad. Sure hope you'll come so you can collect your pay. From what you said, we need you to guide us across the desert and through the mountains."

Horntoad Harry didn't reply, and eventually

they heard Red's horse's hooves pound across hard ground and fade.

"What you going to do?" asked Lance.

"I'd like to stay and help. You both know what I've been doing. You just repeat it. They got to get water and food inside 'em . . . or there's no chance. It'll take real work and care."

"We'll do our best," replied Katy.

"I'm sure you will," said the old man. "Darn it, I reckon Red and those men would suffer without me. Lance, I've taken a fancy to you, feller. Once this is over, will you try to catch up and join us?"

"Maybe. Miss Katy and I haven't talked much. It'll be whatever she says."

"You two make me cry," said Katy, firelight flickering on her shadowed face. "I don't know what to say. If you hadn't come along . . . I'd . . ."

"You keep that lye soap and extra water handy. You got to keep your hands clean after touching 'em. Lance, I'll work to midnight. You think you can take over after that?"

"Yes," replied the big man.

The fire of dried buffalo dung, grass, and sticks, crackled and burned low. The three sat some time before Horntoad Harry lit a lantern and went back to caring for the sick men.

"Miss Katy, we've done all we can for now," said Lance. "I laid out our bedrolls next to the fire."

At midnight, the old man woke Lance. He

130

shook hands with the giant youth, and then thumped him hard on the back.

"When this here is done," whispered Horntoad, "you bring that lady, her kid, your friend and . . . whoever else, up the trail. You and me will meet again. If you got it in you for a partner, I'll be waitin'."

Lance was about to reply when the old man took to his mule and hurried away.

After the frontiersman left, Lance and Katy worked over the sick men, sharing the labor, nearly twenty-four hours a day. They became exhausted from the indelicate work and little sleep.

Fast Eddy watched over Katy's boy. Lance's friend kept the group supplied with boiled water, cooked food, and soup for the sick men. Eddy found it easy to hunt for mule deer and antelope that came to the stream to drink. Following what he learned from Horse and then Horntoad, he salted and jerked large amounts of meat for the future. There were idle moments each day and the caretaker of the young boy soon began to form a bond with the lad.

Uncounted days slipped by and, ill and emaciated, Katy's father Peter Day and her Uncle Harold continued to decline. Both men remained alive only because they were repeatedly given water and soup. It was becoming evident that no matter how carefully they were cared for, the disease was making them steadily weaker. It was only Clare Day who seemed to be holding his own. After two weeks of endless nursing, Katy's father Peter and his brother Harold lost consciousness and both died within hours of each other.

Fast Eddy dug graves, and Katy looked on as the men were buried. Crying, the daughter said words over her father and uncle. Clare was the only one to recover, and was still weak; he sat and watched as his two brothers were buried.

It was a typical warm day, cloudless, with a wide-open blue sky. In the distance a wolf howled and near the stream coyotes yipped and made high-pitched calls in pursuit of some animal. A hot breeze was blowing and tall grass and brush rustled all around them.

With renewed energy, Katy took care of her Uncle Clare as he slowly recovered. The next day she collapsed and immediately developed a fever. The men feared she had come down with cholera. It was several days before they realized that Katy was not vomiting, and that she was merely exhausted. Clare, once the patient, now attended to his niece's intimate needs. Weak himself, he had help from Lance when asked to provide it.

In a week, Katy was eating and she recovered quickly. It was her uncle who needed more time. And while the rest of them prepared for the trip to the California gold fields, he slowly regained his health.

One evening, just before dark, Lance came into camp very dirty, sweating from cutting extra hay for the animals, and gathering dried buffalo dung. There was a canvas spread beneath the one saved wagon and into this, dung was gathered. Knowing there would be no fuel for fire on their trip across the desert, and because there were no trees growing along the river, they were forced to make do with what was available.

Eddy unharnessed the mules and inside the wagon worked at packing down the cut grass.

Lance went behind the water barrels to wash, and when he finished, he donned clean pants and walked towards the camp. Always conscious of his condition, he was about to pull on his shirt when Katy came up beside him. She gasped loudly.

"Lance," she cried out. "What ever happened to you?"

Katy was close now and for the first time in her life she touched him, running her right hand along the mass of scars on his back. Lance side-stepped away from her and quickly pulled on his shirt.

"It's nothing," he said.

"Oh," said Katy. "I've never seen anything like it. Does it hurt?"

"No."

"What happened to you? How . . . I mean . . . what terrible thing has someone done to you?"

"I'd rather not talk about it," replied Lance.

"Don't you trust me? Aren't we friends? Aren't we more than just . . ."

"Of course I trust you."

"You've been so wonderful to me. If it wasn't for you and your friend, maybe all of us would have died. In fact, I've been thinking about it, and I am certain Johnny and I would have gotten sick."

"You would have done the same . . ."

"No, I wouldn't have," replied Katy emphatically. "Like everyone else, I would be afraid of getting sick. Only you, Eddy, and that wonderful old man . . ."

"We were glad to help."

"Now that we're better, are you going to leave?"

"I'll remain as long as you and your uncle need . . . or . . . want me," replied Lance.

"I've already told Uncle Clare that I care about you."

"You did?" he asked, bending his tall frame down so he could hear her soft voice.

"I told him," she whispered hesitantly, "that I would go anywhere you go, as long as you would have us. After all, you saved our lives."

"You needn't say such things," said Lance.

"Oh, but I must. You even gave up going with

134

those other men to the gold fields. Look at how many miners passed by and not one offered to help."

"I think it was what happened in my past . . . that made me . . ."

His declaration even surprised him and he stopped to think about what he just admitted, to himself, as well as to Katy.

While they were talking, the sun set and darkness fell all around them. A hot wind that had been blowing all day, abruptly stopped. Insects chirped loudly. Packs of coyotes beginning their nightly hunt howled. An owl hooted, and the air became cooler and thicker as it seemed to settle down upon them.

"It's time we talked," said Katy. "I never properly thanked you or Eddy. It's almost as if both of you are part of my family."

"I feel the same way."

"Then why be so secretive? You've never told me anything about your past and those scars on your back. There are so many of them. It must have been very painful . . ."

"I'm ashamed," said Lance.

"You don't trust me," said Katy.

"Yes, I do. But you can't possibly want to know where I came from or what I . . ."

There was a long silence. And in that silence, coyote calls filled the night.

"Is it as bad as all that?" asked Katy.

"Worse," replied Lance.

"Tell me then," she said. "Otherwise, it will always stand between us. I just can't imagine you ever deliberately doing anything wrong."

It was a long time before Lance began to speak. For a while, the two of them walked along the stream and then they came to where the mules and horses were picketed. They could hear the tearing and chewing of grass. They walked beyond the sound and out onto dry prairie and shorter grass, far from the river where no one could hear them.

Then slowly, picking his words carefully, Lance told Katy about his past. Several times he heard her gasp, but he continued on, talking faster and the words spilled from him. He told her how he was born, about how he was raised as a slave, and how the black woman known as Mammy was his one constant comfort. He explained that he had lived a life of harsh labor and constant cruelty. When he told of the Sunday readings from the Bible, and of the poverty and conditions he endured, Katy grasped his arm. Lance explained what the woman known as Mammy meant to him and to the other slaves. When he described her death, he relived those emotions and choked with the telling of it.

"Go on," said Katy. "Mammy died and you and the others had to continue . . ."

"Yes," replied Lance. "After that it was never

the same. There was no one to replace her, and life became harder. We tried to meet on Sundays, but none of us could read and all we could do is talk about her and what she had done for us. And then I began to fight back and many times I tried to run, and I was caught and whipped and . . ."

"You've told me enough," said Katy, her voice quavering. "You can tell me more later. The rest I can guess. You escaped and that's why you're here now."

"Yes," said Lance. "Now you know."

"Why did you believe I would think badly of you?" asked Katy. "That was your past, you're a westerner now, just like me. We're on the California Trail and we're headed for the gold fields and a new life. I feel even closer to you. Just imagine . . . all you've been through . . . yet you are the kindest, most gentle man I've ever known."

"You still care for me after all . . . I said?"

"You know I do. I won't ever repeat any of it. You trusted me enough. Now let me share some of my . . ."

They walked further out onto the prairie.

"I've never said this to anyone but perhaps you'll understand me better if I do. My father . . . he tried his best . . . but there were times when he lost his temper. We had a little land and raised cattle and crops. Father always wanted to go west and Mother wouldn't let him. When Mother, my husband, and my uncles' families died from a fever epidemic back in Missouri, my father and my uncles heard of the gold strike, and nothing could stop them. I had no choice but to bring Johnny and go with them."

"Do you miss your husband?" asked Lance.

"You will think I'm terrible, but no," replied Katy.

"What do you mean?" asked Lance, surprise showing in his voice.

"Father liked Jack, my husband. Sometimes I think better than me. Jack worked on the farm and he courted me and Father pushed. I was young and not so sure."

"And you married him?"

"I resisted as long as I could. He and my uncles built us a little cabin. Too late, I found out that Jack had a temper. When he was tired and drinking, he used to hit me. I didn't know what to do and Father was . . ."

"I'm sorry," said Lance, and for the first time in his life, the big man reached out and put his large arms gently around a woman.

It felt natural, and to his surprise Katy did not pull away, but instead hugged him back.

"I'm sorry, too," said Katy, "and most of all I miss my mother. But I suppose . . . no, I *believe* . . . sometimes in this life, things happen for a reason."

"Mammy said that God is always watching

over us, and that He never gives us more than we can handle."

"She must have been a very special lady," said Katy.

"She was everything to me."

The two remained in each other's arms. A pack of coyotes, very close, suddenly began high-pitched howling, followed by constant yipping. This broke the magic of the moment.

"Perhaps we better get back to camp."

"Before we do," said Katy. "I have one last confession."

"Yes?"

"I've seen you once before."

"You did?" asked Lance. "Where?"

"It was on a river. You were unloading a boat and I just couldn't look away. You were so splendidly strong and handsome."

They continued to embrace and both felt the heat of the other through their clothing. Then Lance began to release her, and in that instant Katy stood on tiptoes. He bent lower and she reached up and kissed him hard on the lips.

"There," she said. "I've wanted to do that since the first time I ever saw you."

Along the way in the dark, Katy found and held Lance's hand. When they finally came to the camp, they separated and went up to the fire to greet the others.

CHAPTER TEN

Nearly four weeks passed before supplies and kegs of boiled water were tied on the mules and the wagon. Katy and Johnny rode up on the seat beside Uncle Clare who drove the team. Lance and Fast Eddy each guided six heavily laden mules. Following a map Horntoad Harry had drawn, they left the Humboldt River and headed west across the desert.

It took all day to travel twelve miles, and despite the well fed and rested stock, the desert heat and barren dryness took its toll. Water would not last long under these conditions. They made a dry camp and rested. Early in the morning, after watering the stock and themselves, they continued on. During the middle of the day they came upon two wagons and eight worn out mules. There were six men and they had pushed themselves and their stock since leaving Missouri and all of them were mere skin and bones.

"We'll give you money, guns, anything we have for water," whispered the leader of the group.

Despite the protestations of Fast Eddy and Clare, Lance left two large barrels of water. Several of the men tried to give a twenty dollar gold piece and Lance refused. Then one of the men came forward and into Katy's hand he placed a gold locket and chain.

"It was my wife's. She died and it would be my honor if the pretty lady would take it."

Katy put the necklace in a pocket and then she reined her mules forward. Behind them they heard the thirsty men gather around the two water barrels. A few miles further on, Eddy asked Lance the obvious question.

"Do you think they'll make it?"

"If they leave their wagons, take a couple of mules, and spare the water, they have a chance."

"Do you think they will?"

"No," replied Lance.

Further on, they came upon abandoned furniture, parts of broken-down wagons, bones of dead mules and horses, and several human skeletons. Everything that Horntoad Harry had said about this desert was true. It was harder going than they imagined and at the end of the day, they stopped to save the mules. Many of the water barrels were already empty, and several of them they discarded to lighten the load for the thirsty animals.

They lit a dung fire to heat coffee and warm and soften dried meat. From experience, even upon the desert, the three men shared guard duty.

In the morning, after breakfast, coffee, and watering the stock, they continued on. At midday they saw a group of horses moving diagonally towards them.

"We'll dismount and stand ready," suggested Lance.

Using the vehicle for cover, the men stood with rifles. Katy and little Johnny stayed hidden behind the wagon and water barrels.

"They ride like soldiers," said Clare.

"They saw our fire last night," explained Lance. "We knew better than to light one at dark."

There was a line of eleven horsemen, riding in columns of two. They halted some distance away.

"Hello the wagon!" came a call.

"Who is it?" asked Lance.

"My name's Colonel Stevenson. I mustered out last year. Presently I am the *alcalde* of a little gold town called Moke Hill. Perhaps you've heard of it?"

"No, sir," responded Lance. "I know neither of your town or what an alcalde is."

"I was appointed mayor to draw up a code of mining laws and regulations. The gold is very rich there and it has brought many disputes."

"Then why are you on the desert and with these soldiers?" asked Lance.

"I heard reports that travelers along this stretch were dying. We've been putting up signs at the Humboldt River warning people to fill up with water before crossing the desert. These soldiers were loaned to me for that purpose."

"We had a scout warn us to take plenty of water," said Lance.

"How fortunate for you," replied the colonel. "We're also recruiting miners and laborers to our town—if you are interested. When gold was discovered, President Polk appointed me and had me bring a regiment of men around the horn to California. That's how I happen to be here now."

"You came by boat?"

"Yes, as a matter of fact, half as many are coming by ship. They're calling themselves Argonauts. Would you mind us joining your camp?"

"We're armed, Colonel, and we've had our share of trouble."

"Then you don't believe what I am saying?"

"We prefer to take no chances."

"Then let me tell you, if you make it across this infernal waste, the worst of your trip will be done. You will reach the Carson River and from there, pass over the mountains to California. I recommend you think about coming to our town. Here's a map I'm giving to travelers showing how to find the Carson River, then go south to reach the Mokelumne River. You follow that right into Mokelumne Hill."

Lance took a folded paper and stuck it in his pocket.

"And, I have a great deal more to . . ."

"Colonel," said Lance, "we've faced robbers,

cholera, thirst, and hunger. What more can you warn us about?"

"A great deal more about the mining camps! Perhaps what I have to relate to you will be of importance."

"We're listening."

The leader of the group dismounted and walked forward.

"You can lower your rifles," said Colonel Stevenson. "You have nothing to fear from me."

"If you don't mind, we will keep our guard," said Lance.

The colonel smiled stiffly. "Healthy folks like you are exactly the type our town is calling for," he said, looking up at the big man.

"You said you had something important to tell us," interrupted Clare.

"No need to be rude, Uncle," said Katy.

"Thank you, ma'am, it has been a hard ride, and it is a pleasure to see a woman of such beauty on so barren a plain."

Katy blushed.

"What do you know of the gold fields?" asked Colonel Stevenson.

"Not much," admitted Lance. "We see many men passing along the trail. We heard there's much gold."

"Both true. Already, there are nearly sixty thousand people in the gold camps, and more coming every day. San Francisco is nearly abandoned. Shipping vessels sail in and whole crews desert leaving the boats sitting empty in the harbor. Farmers, ranchers, and merchants have left their jobs for the gold fields and soldiers from some of the forts have deserted. Last year, men in Moke Hill were so busy digging and gathering gold they refused to stop to get supplies. The town and the miners were starving until one fellow went to Stockton and returned with food. It made him rich. There are all kinds of opportunity to make money, and not all of it is digging for gold."

"You're just saying that, mister," said Clare.

"I'm not. And you should know what you're facing before you get there."

"Well, get on with it," said Clare.

"This is what I have seen with my own eyes," said Colonel Stevenson. "If a man is willing to work hard, dig, and move a great deal of earth, gold can be dug out of the rivers and tributaries. I've seen five men on a Long Tom collect a hundred dollars in gold in one day. I've seen thirty-five Indians working to earn clothes and supplies, dig up twelve thousand in nuggets and dust, using willow baskets. I witnessed two miners with a rocker move a hundred yards of dirt from a trench, in a week, and wash out seventeen thousand in gold."

"That's what I'm talking about!" replied Clare, his eyes blazing.

"But with all the land and claims still open, not everyone finds gold. Most men on average dig up twenty-five to thirty-five dollars worth in a day."

"You're trying to scare us off," said Clare.

"Not at all. Thousands have the gold fever and they're coming from everywhere in the world. This is what I'm here to tell you. The real money is not in prospecting but in supplying the miners."

"That can't be true," replied Clare.

"But it is," said the colonel. "I need men to carry food and supplies to the gold camps. Think what good use these mules could be put to. You can get supplies in Stockton and sell to the miners. Why, a pound of sugar is going for two dollars . . . coffee . . . flour. Women are charging twenty-five dollars for a cooked meal. Prices are sky-high—miners with gold will pay almost anything."

"We'll think on it, Colonel Stevenson," said Lance. "We're obliged to you for stopping."

"My pleasure, and now that I think about it, perhaps your distrust along the trail is a wise action. I suggest you continue to be cautious. There's no law and men are robbed and killed every day. Already there have been thousands murdered—not just for gold but for food and supplies. Men are killing Indians in order to strike claims on their land or to steal their women and children for slaves. The law here allows Indian slaves. And the Indians are attacking the miners in reprisal. Any man who goes into the gold fields risks his life in many ways. Those mules of yours, you'll never keep them if you don't stand guard."

"Thanks for warning us, Colonel," said Lance.

"My men and I will move on, we want to get off this accursed desert. Perhaps we will run into each other again. If so, could I have your names?"

"This is Katherine, and I'm Lance."

The well-dressed stranger tipped his hat and mounted. The troop rode directly west and it was a long time before they disappeared from view.

"Do you think he told the truth of it?" asked Clare.

"I do, Uncle," replied Katy.

"Me too," said Fast Eddy.

On the third day, before daylight, they again watered the mules, discarded more empty kegs, and moved on. The group pushed forward into dusk, and still the desert was before them. Not daring to stop, they traveled through the night, climbing higher and into the mountains. Dry barren land turned to grass and the air became cooler. They came to trees and finally to the gurgling and fast-moving Carson River. Exhausted, they made camp. They spent the night on the mountain next to the stream and in the morning rose early, anxious to get to the gold fields.

"You might take that fellow's notion about using the mules for carrying freight, and it might be true it will earn us more money," said Clare. "But I'm not traveling all the way across the country to the gold fields and not try a little gold mining."

"I think we should all have a go at it," said Fast Eddy. "We'd be fools not to at least stake a claim and try. If we don't strike it rich, we can always fall back to hauling freight."

"I'd like to try too," said Katy.

"And me," added Johnny.

"I guess I'm outnumbered but eventually I want to go into the freighting business," replied Lance. "While we're mining, we're gonna have trouble with the mules, feeding them and guarding them."

They ate breakfast, packed up the mules, hitched the wagon, and saddled their horses. They guided the animals along the Carson River, following the sketched map given to them by Colonel Stevenson. After leaving the Carson, they began to travel straight south to attempt to find the northern section of the Mokelumne River. As they passed through forested mountain peaks, heading south, they began to cross over small rivers and streams. Occasionally they caught glimpses of various sized lakes. On the streams they saw roughly dressed miners, with picks and shovels digging out mud and gravel and shoveling into Long Toms, using the rushing water to wash away stones and dirt in an effort to find gold. Other places they saw single men filling pans and washing them in the moving water. These miners were intense in their work and they appeared worn and tired. Each man or group of men seemed deeply focused upon their task, and when seeing the party of travelers, they looked up wild eyed and wary. None of these men were inclined to talk or to step away from their labor. The gleam of long rifles and pistols near the miners revealed their steely cautiousness.

Traveling, they reached the top of one steep incline. Lance, in front leading the first long line of mules, stopped in his tracks. The others behind him did the same. The men, as well as Katy and the boy stared. Before them, coming down the trail was an emaciated man of undetermined age, wearing ragged clothing, worn work boots, no hat, and upon one side of the man's head was a bloody wound. The blood had run down the miner's face and soaked into his torn woolen shirt. Dried now, it was a crusty red. His scalp, his neck, and shirt contained hunks of dried gore. The man staggered as he walked and he appeared a frightful sight. Slowly, the injured man approached and when he was only a few feet away, Lance dismounted and called out to him.

"Sir, you are hurt. Can we help you?"

The man turned glassy-eyed, at first not

appearing to comprehend, and then his eyes seemed to focus and he opened his mouth to speak. His first utterance was a hoarse whisper which made no sense. Then the man cleared his throat and made his response.

"You are speaking to me, sir?"

"I am."

"And you said?"

"You appear to be badly injured," repeated Lance. "May we help?"

"No man on this earth can help me this day," responded the injured man.

By now Katy had dismounted and tied her mount. She came forward with a canteen and handkerchief, her intent to give drink and help clean the terrible wound on the man's head. Young Johnny climbed down from the wagon seat and moved forward. He took a closer look and then stepped back behind a mule. Clare followed Katy, and Fast Eddy stared from some distance, wanting to listen, but like young Johnny having no desire to see more.

"What has happened to you, man?" asked Lance.

"I . . . we . . . my son and I were robbed of our gold."

"You are badly injured," said Lance. "Come, sit down."

There was a deep hole in the man's head. Those in the group could see it and each wondered what the exposed white substance was. The injured man stared glassy-eyed off into space and with a hoarse voice began to speak. Lance took hold of the man's arm and shoulder and gently guided the fellow to the trunk of a large pine tree and sat him down. The man gave no resistance. Once the injured fellow started speaking, it was as if he was in a trance. The whispery voice droned on without stopping. While he spoke, all of the members of Lance's group came closer to listen.

"My son and I worked like dogs. We searched the stream, found color, and staked our claim. We built a Long Tom and started digging. It was sinful what I turned into. Once we started finding gold I went crazy with the fever. Even a lazy man, once finding gold would turn into a worker, and I had been a worker all my life. I barely slept, I barely ate, I cursed the darkness for keeping me from digging. I stood in the cold stream with pickaxe and shovel and dug and dug. I dug till my hands bled. I dug until my legs turned numb and I could no longer stand. Time and again my son had to drag me from the stream and cover me with blankets. Other men around us found gold, too, and they dug as we did, crazy starved men after yellow color. We ran out of food and others did, too. While they sickened and weakened and fell ill, I did not. My son finally went away and came back with supplies. He purchased a mule with his gold and brought back a heavy load. We finally ate well, strengthened, and went back to work."

As the injured man was speaking, buzzing flies began to gather and land on the wound. Lance saw them crawl into the deep hole in the skull and disappear. The man did not seem to notice. Unable to cope with the gruesome sight, Lance began brushing away the flies, and repeated the action all the time the injured fellow was speaking.

"We worked for months, digging down into bedrock. There came a time when Jonathan said we had enough. He worried about a sickness, typhoid or cholera, or some such was bringing down the miners. He kept saying we had enough gold and it was time to go. I argued with my own son. I had the gold fever and I wanted to stay. We fought, I struck him, and then somehow I came to my senses."

For a few brief moments the injured miner quit talking and stared into space. Whatever it was, he slowly raised his hands and arms toward it. They reached out and grabbed hold of something. The old man's face grimaced into horrible anguish and then the arms dropped to his sides. His features once again became expressionless, and the man continued his narrative as if he had never stopped.

"We heard there were highwaymen but we were armed, we left in the middle of the night, loading our mule with our gold, telling no one of our departure. But when we came to the top of the mountain on our way to Stockton and a ship home, three armed men stopped us. One said they were watching our work through a spy glass, and when we no longer were on our claim, they knew we were pulling out. My son Jonathan argued. One of the men shot him. I grabbed my knife and was inches away from the man's back when something struck me hard from behind."

Lance had taken the canteen from Katy, opened the spout, and tried to force the man to drink. Oddly, the fellow pushed the canteen away. Taking the clean handkerchief and soaking it, Lance attempted to dab gently at the man's wound. Again the fellow kept pushing Lance's hand away.

"Why, man," said Lance, "I am trying to help you."

"There is no help for one such as me," replied the injured fellow, in a voice that had no emotion.

"How long has it been since you've eaten?" asked Lance.

"Since my son was killed," responded the wounded stranger.

"How long has that been?"

"Four days."

"Here now!" said Lance. "You must take food and water and let me clean your wound."

"No, now that you have sat me down, I will never get up and walk again."

"Don't talk nonsense," replied Lance. "Once you drink, eat, and rest, you will be fine."

"I will never be fine again," replied the sick man, now in a louder voice. "I will not live much longer."

"Come now," said Lance. "All of us have hardships, you are no exception. Be a man and . . ."

"No. Make no more effort. But now that you are here, let me talk."

"Please," said Katy bending down on one knee and taking up the canteen. "Please, mister, take a drink. It will help you."

"No, miss, it will only prolong my suffering. Don't you see? I am mortally wounded. Maybe you would like to hear my confession?"

"If it will help," replied Katy hesitantly.

"Beware of the Gold Fever!" blurted out the man, whose eyes once again appeared glassy and unfocused.

"Yes?" said Katy, not knowing what else to say.

"It was I who talked my son Jonathan into leaving our ranch in Texas. After my wife died, my son and I struggled to keep up the place. We worked hard but had little. Still, we enjoyed each other's company. But then I read of the gold strike, the desire set in, and I started talking. At first he didn't want to leave, but then we took what little money we had and came north. We ran our horses to skin and bone. And when we arrived . . . well . . . I told you that part."

"Please, take this water," said Katy.

"Don't you see?" blurted out the man in fierce anguish. "I killed my son!"

"Mister," replied Lance, "we have all faced grief. Believe me, I know. But that is no reason for you to lie down and die."

"For me it is . . ." began the injured fellow, and then the man's head slumped heavily.

Lance came to his knees and felt the man's neck, then stood up and moved away.

"Fast Eddy, Clare, grab a shovel and that pickaxe."

"He can't be dead," exclaimed Katy.

"But he is," replied Lance. "Strange that he lived this long. That hole in his skull should probably have killed him. The man was clear out of his mind."

"Never heard a fellow so bent on dying," commented Clare.

They stayed long enough to dig a deep hole, bury the man, and say a few words over the dead fellow. It was a sober group that returned to the trail. The words of the dead man lingered with all of them. When evening came they camped at the edge of some trickling brook, and everyone in the party spoke little, ate their supper in silence, and turned into their bedrolls early. Lance took the first guard, making sure the horses and mules were secure. As he paced slowly around camp, he vowed that it was better to serve others.

Old Horntoad Harry had it right, thought Lance. *Grubbing in the dirt is no way to make a living.*

In the morning they moved on and they traveled for days, occasionally asking directions from the taciturn miners until they were sure they had found the northern branch of the Mokelumne River. This they followed towards the town of Moke Hill. As they journeyed further southwest, they came upon hundreds of miners spread out on claims on either side of the river. These miners stared at the wagon, horses, and mules with obvious envy. When they arrived at a likely bend with no claim or miner to be seen, Clare called a halt, climbed down from the wagon, and took a pan and pointed to the curve in the stream.

"You all got to understand that my brothers gave up their farms, their lives, to come here in search of gold. I just got to stop and try mining. Lance, there's grass for animals, and a likely place to build a camp. I say we stop."

"Looks good to me," added Fast Eddy.

"Aren't you going to try to look for color first?" asked Lance.

"Them other fellers upstream staked claims," replied Clare. "I bet they didn't do it for no reason."

Lance pulled the mules into a circle, and began unloading supplies.

"Yahoo!" shouted Clare, and Fast Eddy joined in.

The two men took their gold pans and ran to the edge of the stream. They dipped them in the mud and then began sloshing it around as they had seen other miners do. It was not as easy as it looked and took practice and time before the mud left the pan.

"I got some dust!" shouted Clare.

Eddy was still busy sloshing, and Katy and Johnny ran down to look in their uncle's pan. What they saw were a few tiny specks of gold.

"How do you get it out, Uncle Clare?" asked Johnny.

"It would take a long time to turn that into an ounce," commented Katy.

"Well, it's a start!" exclaimed Clare.

Katy and Johnny found a third pan and Johnny dragged a shovel and Katy a pickaxe down to the stream. Johnny stepped on some rocks and with the shovel managed to dig down and come up with gravel and mud. This they placed in the pan and then they added water, and together, awkwardly, the two began moving the pan back and forth, using the water to force the lighter mud out over the pan's rim. When all the mud was gone, they picked through and tossed out the larger stones, and pebbles. After one more load of water, and careful sloshing, they found several specks of gold and one very tiny nugget.

Johnny, with forefinger and thumb, picked out the nugget.

"Now what do we do with it?"

Katy had a small glass bottle for that purpose and she pulled the cork stopper and her son placed the nugget in it. It made a small tinkling sound as it hit the bottom of the glass. Katy tried to pick out the gold flecks in the bottom of the pan without success. Johnny tried, too, and failed. While Katy worked at it, Johnny picked up the gold bottle and ran to Lance to show him their very first nugget.

Lance had unloaded the mules. In his hand he had an axe and he had already chopped down a small tree and was busy trimming off branches. He finished just when Johnny arrived. Lance bent down and stared hard to see the little nugget.

"Good job," said Lance. "Now go do it again!"

"What about you?" asked the boy.

"I got to fix things up around camp," replied the big man. "I suppose my search for gold can start tomorrow or the next day. If you don't want to dig, you make a claim by building two cairns of rocks, like we saw those other miners had. Make it from over near the bend to back where your uncle is. Your uncle can cross the stream, and make two cairns on the other side."

The rest of the day everyone stayed busy at

their own tasks. Johnny put up the rock cairns as Lance had instructed. Katy, Clare, and Fast Eddy worked at panning gold and by nightfall their findings were meager, with a few specks and grains that had hardly any value. Lance had tied three large limbs between evenly spaced trees and over the limbs he placed canvas, creating three tents. The ends he pegged to the ground. He pulled down the sides of the canvas and secured them. The wagon was for Johnny and Katy to sleep in. The three tents were for the men. They would keep out rain and wind, but not the cold. Near the tents Lance hauled rocks and formed a cooking area.

Lastly, a corral was built by Lance for the mules and horses. One end extended close to the water. He dug a ditch with pickaxe and shovel and water seeped in, allowing the animals drink without having to leave the enclosure. A strong corral was created of logs tied to living trees and a movable gate was nailed together and roped to trees. Lance used his powerful muscles all day and by evening he was tired. Before turning in, he warned the others that the mules would have to be guarded closely from theft, and in the near future they would have to cut grass for hay. Before falling asleep, Lance got up once more from the tent he had built for himself.

"That man who told us about the robbery, said people were watching. Maybe some thieves are up in the mountains spying on us and others along this river. I want every one of you to have your rifles loaded and near. No telling who will come to rob or steal our supplies or mules. I don't know, but we might have to fight to keep what we have. Out here there's only us to protect ourselves. In the morning, I'll place rock formations around the camp to shoot behind."

"Aren't you going a bit far with that?" said Clare.

"Maybe," replied Lance. "But ever since we met that fellow, I've had a feeling, and I'm not going to ignore it. There was a reason that old man lived long enough to tell us his story. By rights, that awful wound should have killed him dead. You can believe what you want, but I think he was sent to warn us. All of you keep your guns loaded, close, and ready."

The next morning the camp was awakened by a gunshot.

Lance sat up from his bedroll, pulled on boots, grabbed his pistol and rifle, and ran from his tent. He headed towards where he thought the shot came from. Fast Eddy was standing behind a tree near the corral, and the stock was huddled at one end in a bunch.

"What happened?" asked Lance.

"Just before daylight the mules got restless," said Fast Eddy. "I came down to the corral and I saw several dark figures at the other side, doing something. There was enough starlight that I saw a flash. A fellow cut some rope and one end of a log came loose. I aimed and fired and . . ."

"Good job," replied Lance. "I told you we're going to have to keep guard. That colonel said our mules are worth a fortune out here."

Together, Eddy and Lance walked around the corral. The stock continued to stay huddled together in a bunch. When they came to the fallen log, in the light of the rising sun, footprints of several men could be seen in the dirt. The rope securing one end of the fencing to a living tree was cut with a knife.

"Look!" said Lance. "There's blood and the knife."

Whoever had cut the rope was struck by Eddy's bullet and had dropped the knife as he ran. Together Eddy and Lance followed tracks, their rifles at the ready. When they came to trees and heavy brush, they found where horses had been tied, and where shod hooves tore up the ground.

"There were three or more," said Lance. "Come on, let's get back to camp and eat breakfast. Just like I said, we've got mules and a lot of supplies. If we're to keep them, we'll have to guard both day and night."

"What about gold mining?" asked Fast Eddy.

"I'll leave that up to you and Clare, but you'll have to do your share of guarding."

"I didn't think it was going to be like this," said Fast Eddy.

"I'm afraid that a lot of those who find gold don't always get too far with it."

Everyone at camp was up and dressed. Clare and Katy were carrying rifles. Fast Eddy told them what happened.

At the moment the sun cleared the horizon, from a distance they saw a group of travelers move across the trail before them. Lance and his party held rifles and suspiciously eyed the strangers until they passed from view.

"How can a feller do any mining?" asked Clare, with disgust in his voice.

"Clare, I want you to stand guard while I build something to protect us," said Lance.

"What are you thinking?" asked Katy.

"We're out in the open here. I'm thinking of building a rock wall in case we come under attack, we'll have something to hide behind."

"There's certainly plenty of rocks," said Johnny.

What would have taken several men days to move and haul, Lance accomplished in one. By the end of the second day, carefully fitting rocks together, and at times using clay mud to secure the stones, Lance built a wall four feet high and six feet long. Then he spent several more days improving this structure by adding more rocks with spaces in between to use when firing. Behind the wall he dug a wide trench, a foot deep. At the ends of the wall he placed more rocks for cover.

On the fifth day, Lance sat down to supper, satisfied with his work.

"That's the best I can think of," said Lance.

"Just think how much gold we could have found by now, if you had used all that energy in the stream," commented Clare.

"He did it to protect us, Uncle," said Katy smiling. "I think it was very . . ."

"Smart!" said Johnny.

"I think it was a big waste of time," said Clare. "No one would be foolish enough to attack us. More like before, when they come sneaking around in the dark."

"That's why we have to guard," said Lance. "We have to keep Katy and Johnny safe, too."

"What I want to know is when you're going to help us dig?" asked Fast Eddy.

"This was our best day yet. We found nearly an ounce of gold. The deeper we go into the stream, the more we find. Too bad we didn't bring boards to build a rocker."

"Lance, will you help us mine tomorrow?" asked Katy. "You can't come all this way and not look for gold."

"All right," said Lance. "But while I'm digging, Clare or Fast Eddy have to guard."

"I can do the guarding tomorrow," said Katy.

"You know I can shoot and give warning just as well as they can."

That night Lance stood guard to midnight and then woke Eddy. The big man turned in and as tired as he was, he did not fall asleep for some time. Just like the colonel had told him, there were thousands coming to the gold fields on ships and by land. There was no law and nothing to keep armed men from taking what they wanted. That poor fellow with the horrible wound had warned them. Lance lay in his bedroll and worried. He would never forgive himself if something happened to Katy or little Johnny.

At dawn, Lance was up and checked with Clare who had final guard. There was nothing to report, except a party of miners who went by before daylight. They had breakfast and as the sun rose, Lance used his enormous strength to move gravel and mud. Since they had no Long Tom or gold rocker, Lance simply piled what he dug up on the shore of the stream. Here, Johnny, Clare, and Fast Eddy could fill their pans, and wash for gold. Lance chose one spot in the gravel next to the shore and began to dig deep. Soon he had a hole several feet down and the cold water rushed over his legs. He worked until he could no longer stand the numbing pain.

"Look what we got with those last few shovelfuls," exclaimed Clare, showing Lance a pan with yellow color all across its bottom.

Carefully extracting the gold from the pan and placing it in a bottle, Clare picked up the shovel Lance had been using and rushed into the stream to begin digging. Clare worked enthusiastically for nearly half an hour, and then exhausted, shivering with cold, he came out of the water to sit on the bank to rest and warm his numb body.

It was like that the rest of the day; Clare, Fast Eddy, and Lance digging in the cold stream and depositing each shovelful on the shore for them to take turns washing for gold. Johnny did his part as well. Most of the gold dust came from deeper shovelfuls of mud and gravel. At the end of the day, due to Lance's enormous effort of moving dirt, they had more gold than ever before.

"I'd say we got two ounces," said Clare, "maybe sixty dollars worth. If we do that every day, in a month, we'll have some real money."

"That would work out to about eighteen hundred," said Fast Eddy, figuring it in his head.

"Sure is a lot of work," said Johnny. "The water's so cold, I couldn't stay in it as long as the three of you did."

"Lance did the most work," said Katy. "I was watching."

"He does as much as the two of you," said Johnny pointing to Clare and Eddy.

"Watch your manners, kid," growled Uncle Clare.

"He's right," said Katy. "I never thought gold mining was so much work."

"Just think," complained Clare. "If we only had a Long Tom to wash the gold, how much faster we could work."

"We'll stay another week," said Lance, "and then we'll go to Moke Hill and find the mayor. You know, that Colonel Stevenson. The way I got it figured, we can earn a lot more money carrying freight than we can standing in a cold stream all day. More than eighteen hundred a month."

"I'm staying," said Clare. "We just started finding color."

"Uncle Clare!" exclaimed Katy. "You wouldn't break away from us? Not after all that we've been through?"

"We finally make it here and find gold and you want to leave?" exclaimed Clare. "I'm working this claim until there's no more gold to find."

"That'll take two years at this rate," said Fast Eddy. "Clare, why don't you stay and watch the claim and let us return with boards to build a Long Tom, then you can really get some work done."

"I don't think it's safe here," said Lance. "I got a bad feeling and I want to take Katy and Johnny to town and talk to the mayor. I've been thinking on it. I want the two of them where there's some law, or soldiers to watch out over them."

"Shouldn't you discuss that with us first?" asked Katy. "We're just as safe as . . ."

"That's it," replied Lance. "I don't think any of us are safe out here. There's not enough of us to stand guard. Not with thousands of dollars worth of mules to steal."

"I think you fret too much over nothin'," said Clare.

"I don't know," said Fast Eddy. "Lance and me have been through a lot and if he doesn't think it's safe I think we ought to listen."

"Whether you go or not, Clare," said Lance, "in another week we'll pack up and head to Moke City. I still say there's not enough of us to fight off an attack."

"Then go!" shouted Clare. "But I'm not leaving this claim!"

The rest of the week the men divided their time between guard duty and mining. Everyone worked hard and due to the back-breaking work and lack of sleep, each of them lost weight. The strain showed on their faces and they began to take on the appearance of the many bone-weary, sharp-eyed miners they first saw. And each time a party of men passed by on the trail before them, they held rifles at the ready.

As before, the more dirt they moved and the deeper they dug, the more gold dust they found. Occasionally there was a nugget or two. Then in mid-week, while Johnny and the three men were at the stream digging and panning for gold, a shot rang out. The sound of galloping horses approaching from the trail could easily be heard.

"To the wall!" shouted Lance, and without waiting for the others, he gathered up his guns and ran.

The big man hurried toward the sound of the single shot and he saw Katy standing near a tree trying to reload her rifle. Men on horses were not more than fifty yards distant and they began shooting. Lance ran calling for the young woman.

"Katy!"

She looked toward him but kept reloading. Lance continued running and he bent down and with one arm scooped up the woman he loved and turned and ran back in the direction of the wall. Katy still had a firm grasp on her rifle but had dropped her powder horn and bullet pouch.

"Look what you made me do!" exclaimed Katy.

Unceremoniously, Lance dumped Katy into the trench behind the barrier. Going to a gap in the stone wall, Lance laid down two holsters with Colt Dragoons, raised his rifle, aiming at the leader, and fired. The thief was struck, and he bent low on his mount. The galloping horse veered sharply and the man fell. By now, Clare and Fast Eddy were behind the wall with Johnny, and they each fired a rifle. Katy moved near to Clare and using his powder, shot, and percussion caps, began to reload. Both Eddy and Lance raised their heavy .44 Colts and continued firing at the mounted men as they charged towards the wall. Too late, the thieves recognized the significance of the barricade. The charging riders turned to either side. Lance fired steadily at the men before him and Fast Eddy did the same. Shooting at the armed men on running horseback was not an easy task. Men were struck, others they missed, and as quickly as the attack started, it was over. They could hear horses running down the trail and away from camp.

"It was the Colts that did it!" exclaimed Fast Eddy, kissing the barrel of his pistol. "Without these beauties, we would have been goners for sure."

"Katy!" shouted Lance. "What were you thinking standing behind that tree? Why didn't you run for cover?"

"I thought I had time . . ." began Katy.

"I saw it," said Johnny. "Lance picked you up and . . ."

"Everybody pack up!" ordered Lance. "We're leaving right now."

"Don't you want to see who we shot or if there are any wounded?" asked Eddy.

"Everybody reload your guns," said Lance. "Eddy, you go check. Clare, Katy, keep me covered while I go get the mules and horses."

Without waiting to see if his orders were being followed, Lance grabbed his second Colt and holster and buckled it around his waist. Then he headed straight for his tent. Inside he picked up some halters and rope and ran for the corral. As he came near the enclosure, he saw a mule lying on the ground. Moving quickly toward it, he saw crimson on the animal's back. It had been shot through the spine and was dead. The other mules and horses were huddled together at the far end of the corral. Lance moved forward and with some difficulty finally caught and haltered one animal. Using the lasso, he continued catching and haltering the mules. He would bridle the horses after the mules had their packs loaded and tied down.

It took time to clear camp, take down the tents, load supplies, and tie the mule train together. Clare saddled the horses and hitched the remaining mules to the wagon. Fast Eddy had time to search the dead. He came back to camp holding a heavy money belt.

"This is off the leader you shot," said Eddy. "Tonight we can count it."

"How many?" asked Lance.

"Two dead men, and one dead horse," explained Fast Eddy. "Plenty of blood from the wounded. I'd say they won't be back any time soon."

"Doesn't matter," replied Lance. "Soon as you help pack up, we're leaving."

Not to the surprise of anyone, Clare helped with the packing. When they were ready, it was

Clare himself who climbed up on the wagon and led the party away from the mining claim. This time Katy rode in the back of the wagon. She had the money belt and counted gold and silver coins. It was a little over five hundred dollars.

The further they followed the Mokelumne River towards the town of Moke Hill, the more miners they saw. Coming to high ground they looked down and before them was a veritable city of tiny hovels on both sides of the stream. Thousands of miners were packed close together, on small placer claims. They labored intently at pulling mud and gravel from the streambed and washing it for color. As Lance's party advanced down the trail they passed by miners from many different countries, all laboring under the hot sun. Traveling through the large encampment, they saw tents, little shacks built of stone, wood, and sticks. There were open fires burning. Pots, pans, and kettles were cooking food, and smoke and various aromas wafted in the air.

Men, women, and children of many races, dressed in subdued colors, blended together as they toiled over their mining claims. The well-practiced labor of thousands created a constantly moving scene for Lance's party to behold. There were groups of Chinese in their strange clothing, wearing round peaked hats, working oddly shaped wooden rockers. On one side of the river, opposite the other miners, were families of blacks digging and mining gold. Close to them was another group of men speaking in a strange language. As they passed by, some of the miners looked up and stared, while others kept at their work without notice. Sunlight gleamed off the stocks and steel barrels of weapons each miner kept within easy reach.

Coming to the bottom of the stream they came upon a group of white men, roughly dressed and heavily armed. Some of them had whips and they were cracking them and shouting at a long line of Indian women and children. The slaves were laboring to carry baskets of ore and dump it in a very large Long Tom, placed in the rushing water. Some of the women had steel shackles and chains attached to their wrists, and when one of them didn't move fast enough, a white guard came forward and cracked his whip at the unfortunate.

Every available space up and down the river was filled with miners, and it was a surprising sight to see so many laboring to dig yellow metal from the rushing river bed. Katy and Johnny both watched the slaves, and they were shocked to see whips used on the Indians. Thankfully they passed quickly up the trail and into the town of Moke Hill. This place, too, was crowded with humanity. Lance, leading the group, stopped the mules in front of the Mayor's office. He climbed down from his horse and stretched his cramped muscles.

"Katy, Johnny, maybe it's best you come with me. Eddy, Clare, stay and watch the animals."

Katy and Johnny climbed down from the wagon. Before they had a chance to enter the building, the mayor came out onto the boardwalk. Two uniformed soldiers followed him, the same two soldiers Lance had seen on the desert trail weeks before.

"You've come!" said the colonel. "Now let me recall . . . Miss Katherine and Lance."

"You remember, Colonel Stevenson," replied Lance.

"Who could forget so charming a lady and so large a man?" said the colonel. "Suppose you call me Mayor Stevenson, in that I have given up my commission. I see you still have the mules."

"I'm afraid we're one short," replied Lance.

"Did you have trouble?" asked the mayor.

"We did."

"Mayor Stevenson," said Katy. "Back there, we saw women chained and men with whips."

"A terrible thing, this slavery of Indians," replied the mayor. "It's Spanish law and now that this territory is in US hands, I'm afraid there are certain white men pushing to pass a law allowing it to continue."

"But they were women and children!" exclaimed Katy.

"Yes, I have seen it with my own eyes. At the present, ma'am, I'm afraid there is nothing the

173

soldiers can do to stop it. You see, California was just taken over from Mexico."

"It's not right," said Katy.

"Slavery is never right," said Lance.

"No, but for the moment, it remains legal," replied Stevenson.

"Mayor," said Lance, "we came to ask about freighting."

"You've come to save the day, sir," said the mayor enthusiastically. "All those miners you passed on the way into town are virtually starving. The food supplies are used up and we're in desperate need. Come into my office and I'll give you a map to Stockton, and I personally will hand you gold to help purchase as much as you can pack and carry back here. Prices are rising every moment we speak. You will be hard pressed to find, and afford to pay for, supplies. Ships that were supposed to haul goods arrive, and crews desert to the gold fields before they are even unloaded. Without sailors, the ships lie and rot in the harbors or are taken over by the town and used in various ways. Thousands are coming by land and sea and we can't keep order."

"Will I have guards?" asked Lance.

"No, sir. I can't afford to go without the few soldiers we have here. But I'll tell you this, if you make it back with supplies, you'll be handsomely rewarded."

Lance and Stevenson went in the building and

when they came out, the big man was holding a canvas bag of gold, a paper supply list, and a map showing the way to Stockton.

"What about Katy and the boy?" asked Lance. "Could I leave them here under your guard?"

"Why, certainly," replied the mayor. "We would . . ."

"Johnny and I won't stay!" said Katy firmly. "I am going wherever you go. Whatever happens, we want to be with you."

"Katy," said Lance. "It's not safe."

"I think," replied Katy, "we'll be safer with you than anyone else."

Within an hour of arriving at Moke Hill, Lance's party changed direction and were soon headed west for the town of Stockton.

CHAPTER ELEVEN

Fast Eddy and Lance had spent enough time with the frontiersmen Horse and Horntoad Harry to know that a guard should always be posted. No matter how tired they were, there was no excuse not to do what was necessary. It was Clare who was awakened by Eddy in the early morning hours to finish guarding, and he failed to stay awake.

When Lance finally awoke, he reached for his holster and belt, which lay close beside him. When he pulled it near, there was no weight to it, and his heavy Colt Dragoon was gone.

Abruptly Lance sat up in his bedroll and before him were three armed men, and one of them was Blacky.

"Looking for this?" asked Blacky.

Yellow teeth flashed as the grinning thug pointed Lance's Colt directly at him.

"Eddy!" shouted Lance.

The loud call woke every member of the camp. Fast Eddy sat up to find himself staring into the barrel of a rifle. Clare, who had been sitting on a keg, had fallen asleep with his back against a tree. He awoke and there was a tough outlaw pointing his own rifle at him. Katy sat up from her bedroll, and seeing the three armed men, immediately reached for her son who was sleeping beside her.

Clare knew he had violated the one rule of guard duty, never to fall asleep. These were tough-looking men and it was his fault they had entered camp.

"Give me my rifle back!" demanded Clare.

The outlaw before him swiped down with the rifle barrel and it struck Clare hard on the top of his head. It knocked him from the keg he was sitting on and to the ground. The blow was hard enough to break open his scalp and blood welled up. He remained on the ground holding a hand to his wound.

"Do you know how long we've been here?" asked the dark-bearded man. "You folks sure do sleep sound."

"What do you want?" asked Lance, shoving back blankets and coming to his stockinged feet.

"Careful," said Blacky. "We don't want that pretty lady over there to be harmed before she has to . . ."

Lance launched his entire body at Blacky. Taken by surprise, the tough man reacted too late. Lance was upon him, one large hand clamped down on Blacky's wrist. He squeezed hard and the revolver fell from the brigand's hand. Blacky roared loudly and took hold of Lance's shirt. Reaching down with his left, Lance grabbed the man's belt and lifted him into the air. When he was shoulder height, Lance threw him. Blacky, still holding the shirt, ripped it from Lance's body revealing rippling muscles, large biceps, and a massively scarred back.

The outlaw next to Clare turned to shoot, and Clare, stone in hand, rose up and crushed the man's skull. He was dead before he hit the ground. Clare picked up the fallen rifle but was too late. The other outlaw fired his weapon and the bullet grazed Lance's left side. A long stripe of red appeared and blood gushed. Then Clare aimed and fired, and the second gunman was struck in the center of his chest and he fell. Fast Eddy, on his feet now, ran to aid his friend. Blacky was already standing and advancing on Lance, knife in hand.

"Eddy! Save Lance!" screamed Katy, who had picked up her son and was carrying him across the camp and away from the fight.

Fast Eddy turned, stooped down, and grabbed a rifle from the man Clare had shot. Rifle raised and aimed, Eddy was afraid to fire. Blacky and Lance were twisting and turning in a lunging knife fight. Lance had retrieved his blade by scooping up his belt and pulling his knife from its sheath.

"I'm going to gut you like a pig!" shouted Blacky.

"You can try," replied Lance, reaching and swiping with the tip of his knife.

It made contact and cut a swath across Blacky's

coat and shirt, and blood dribbled. He jerked back and looked down. "You're going to pay for that," he roared, "that was my favorite coat."

The outlaw lunged with his long knife. The sharp tip sliced across Lance's muscular chest. A long line of red appeared and Katy screamed.

"The pretty lady seems to care," laughed Blacky. "Wait till she sees that face of yours all cut up."

"You talk big for a sneaking coward," said Lance.

Blacky growled and lunged forward with his knife. It made contact, and again blood dripped from a gouge in Lance's ribs, and once more Katy screamed.

"Stop him!" shouted Katy. "Shoot that man!"

"I can't," replied Fast Eddy. "I might hit Lance."

Little Johnny, fully awake, eyes wide, was held tightly against his mother's body. Fast Eddy held the rifle up, aimed and ready to shoot. Clare had found shot, powder, and caps, and was busy reloading his spent rifle. Then into camp came running a buckskinned old man, rifle in hand.

"Don't shoot!" shouted Horntoad Harry.

"How'd you get here?" asked Eddy, his face an expression of surprise.

"Been searching for you everywhere, what took you folks so long? I been jerkin' meat to sell to the miners."

"Can't you see Lance is in danger?" cried Katy. "Do something!"

Horntoad made a cackling laugh. "I knew that sidewinder Blacky would show up. Wouldn't miss this fight for a barrel of gold."

"Please," begged Katy. "Help Lance."

"Don't worry, that big feller can take care of himself. Hey, Lance! Red and the boys built two Long Toms and on the third day started taking gold out of a stream. I hung around long enough to collect some small nuggets to show you folks, and to gather my pay. I went to Stockton, had a fancy dinner, and slept in a bed. It's nearer the gold camps and ships can come up the San Joaquin River and right into the city. Easier than going all the way back to San Francisco for supplies."

The two big men were circling, each holding crimsoned knives. Both fighters had long slices across chest and arms and both were dripping blood.

"You don't know what willpower it took for me not to slit your throat while you was sleepin'!" growled Blacky.

"You should have taken the chance!" replied Lance.

"I know it!" shouted Blacky. "No matter, if it's the last thing I do, I'm gonna slice you open and cut out your heart!"

Blacky lunged and Lance parried, solid steel

striking hard in a metallic clang. Light flashed on the two blades, and everyone watching gasped.

"Cut out his gizzard, boy!" shouted Horntoad and then the old man laughed.

"Oh, how could you?" exclaimed Katy.

Again the old man cackled.

"Boy!" shouted Horntoad. "You cut that mean black-hearted feller up good, 'cause you, me, and the rest of your friends, are going into the meat and supply business. There's thousands and thousands of prospectors grubbin' in the dirt for gold and every one of 'em is starvin' for food and supplies. We're gonna be paid in nuggets and dust and later we can all set up to be the richest ranchers this side of San Francisco!"

"We were heading for Stockton to buy supplies," said Clare. "We got a contract with Moke City."

"Well, when that contract's done, we'll go into freightin' for ourselves. We'll be real en-tre-pre-neurs! Did you hear that, Lance?"

"I'm a bit busy at the moment, Horntoad," replied Lance.

"Shut up, you fool!" exclaimed Blacky. "I'm gonna end your life, you big straw-haired giant!"

Blacky charged forward with his longer knife and the tip cut into Lance's belly. Lance grunted, sidestepped, and stabbed with his shorter knife. The tip went deep into the bicep of the dark-bearded man. Blacky winced and his knife hand dropped. Lance stepped forward and plunged his blade into Blacky's chest. The outlaw jerked back and the knife remained buried, deep in the bad man's heart. Somehow Blacky remained on his feet. With effort he raised his head and eyes to Lance's.

"I thought you was trouble for me, first time I laid eyes on you."

Then Blacky's knees bent and he fell heavily onto his back. Blood poured from his chest and in the silence everyone in the camp heard the long slow sigh of escaping air.

"I knew it!" shouted Horntoad Harry. "Folks . . . happy days are ahead for us!"

ABOUT THE AUTHOR

Charlie Steel, Tale-Weaver Extraordinaire, is a novelist and internationally published author of short stories. Steel credits the catalyst for his numerous books and hundreds of short stories to be the result of being a voracious reader, along with having worked at many varied and assorted occupations. Some of his experiences include service in the Army, labor in the oil fields, in construction, in a foundry, and as a salvage diver. Early in his life he was recruited by the US Government and spent five years behind the Iron Curtain. Steel's work has been recognized and reviewed by various publications and organizations including *Publishers Weekly*, Western Fictioneers, and Western Writers of America. Steel holds five degrees including a PhD. He continues to read, research, and collect western literature. He is the author of *Desert Heat, Desert Cold, and Other Tales of the West*. Charlie Steel lives on an isolated ranch at the base of Greenhorn Mountain, in Southern Colorado.

www.charliesteel.net

Center Point Large Print
600 Brooks Road / PO Box 1
Thorndike, ME 04986-0001 USA

(207) 568-3717

US & Canada:
1 800 929-9108
www.centerpointlargeprint.com